THE SWORD
IN THE
STONE

THE
IN THE

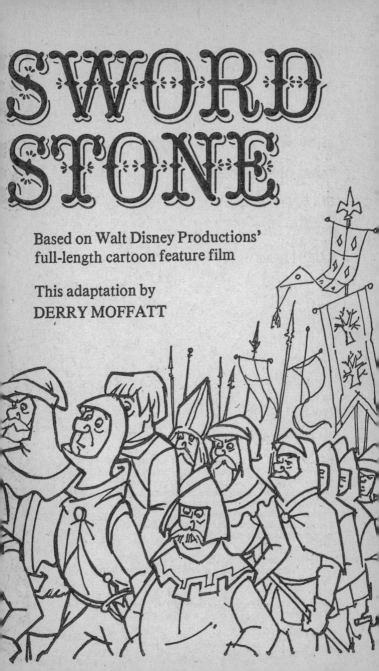

SWORD
STONE

Based on Walt Disney Productions'
full-length cartoon feature film

This adaptation by
DERRY MOFFATT

Other stories from Disney cartoon feature films and available in the NEL series

DUMBO

LADY AND THE TRAMP

SNOW WHITE AND THE SEVEN DWARFS

SONG OF THE SOUTH

SLEEPING BEAUTY

PINOCCHIO

ROBIN HOOD

FIRST NEL PAPERBACK EDITION JANUARY 1976

NEL Books are published by The New English Library Limited from Barnard's Inn, Holborn, London E.C.1. Made and printed in Great Britain by Hunt Barnard Printing Ltd, Aylesbury, Bucks. Typesetting by Yale Press Ltd, London SE25

4500 2807 0

THE SWORD
IN THE
STONE

INTRODUCTION

A legend is sung, of when England was young,
And knights were brave and bold,
The good king had died,
And no one could decide
Who was rightful heir to the throne:
It seemed that the land
Would be torn by war,
Or saved by a miracle alone,
And that miracle happened
In London town . . .
The sword in the stone!

From the shadows of the distant past emerges the story of a bright young boy who grew up to become a famous, much-loved king. Through long centuries the tale has retained its brilliance, never fading or growing dim. The world is full of daydreamers - the vivid imaginings of children's alert minds; their fantasies of being prince or playboy . . . princess or celebrity. Whatever young Arthur's daydreams were, he certainly did not imagine that one day he was destined to rule over a kingdom. But life is full of unexpected twists of Fate, and when you are lucky enough to have a magician as a friend and counsellor, then anything can happen.

England in those remote days was without a king to rule over her. The nobles quarrelled amongst themselves gathering together individual armies to march against each other. Greedy, unscrupulous men added to the turmoil and distress increased with the passing seasons. The country was under a dark cloud . . . an age without law and order. Men lived in fear of one another, afraid to speak their minds, and the strong preyed upon the weak. With so many ambitious men hankering to be king the situation was explosive, as dangerous as a dry tinder box. Intense rivalries and petty jealousy cut deep, and cunning schemes brewed in secret meeting-places. Fanatical plans were discussed.

As yet, young Arthur was unaware of the state of torment that dominated the pleasant countryside. He had the misfortune to be an orphan for both his parents had died when he was little more than a baby. Although he was the son of a king, Uther Pendragon, this fact was wrapped in secrecy. For his own safety his birth was not made known to the majority. Dishonest men without conscience would not have hesitated to do away with the child to further their own aims.

At a tender age Arthur was handed over to Sir Ector, a knight who lived in a castle with his son, Kay. So Kay and Arthur grew up together as brothers. The years slipped by and Arthur grew into a pleasant-faced boy with flaxen hair and bright blue eyes. Kay was red-haired and the taller of the two. He took pride in being first in everything but Arthur didn't mind. He loved Kay and often overlooked his hot temper and impetuous ways.

Although Arthur was unaware of the fact, in faraway London a miracle had occurred. Merlin the magician had caused a large stone to appear beside a church. Upon the stone was an anvil and thrust deep into the anvil was a sword. The sword was named 'Excalibur' and gleamed with a fierce brilliance, dazzling its beholders. Below the hilt in letters of gold were written the words 'Who so pulleth out this sword of this stone and anvil is rightwise King born of England.'

Crowds flocked to London to gaze in awe at the spectacle and many tried in vain to remove the sword from the stone. Men grew angry when their efforts failed, for no one could make it move even the tiniest fraction. Journeying to see the magic sword became a pilgrimage for many and they cheerfully travelled weary miles to gaze and wonder.

In those far off days, London was no more than a village. Black-timbered houses and stone cottages huddled together in confusion and long plumes of smoke drifted from bonfires burning on the village outskirts. Behind the houses, small patches of ground had been tilled and planted with crops, so that they resembled squares on a patchwork quilt. The river, later to be known as the Thames, wound its way through London's village and far beyond - a wide silvery ribbon carrying barges on its restless waters. Many vessels were laden with earth which was transported to fill in the marshy areas which abounded in those days.

The London village was a lively place and since the miracle of the sword, the crowds had increased. Inns and taverns offered welcome refreshment to weary, mud-stained travellers and the thirsty revellers who lived within the village were only too happy to find an excuse to quaff deep draughts of mead and ale with the visitors. Jovial landlords served flagons of foaming beer with a breezy manner. It was one business which seldom lacked custom. The narrow streets wafted a variety of odours, not all of them savoury, yet a breeze blowing gently from the heaths carried the fragrance of the open countryside into the crowded streets.

Beyond the outskirts of London, a vast sheet of scrub, fields and woodland stretched for many miles. A wide variety of trees grew in the woods: oak, ash, birch, willow, yew, hazel, aspen and elm. Wattle and daub thatched cottages dotted the countryside. A number of small, mean, wood and plaster dwellings were built in clusters on the edge of forest clearings, roughly fortified against attacks from wolves which roamed freely over vast areas.

This was the London to which countless men continued to make the hazardous journey in the hope of moving the miraculous sword. None could stir it. To many it seemed that the miracle had not worked - and never would! The country remained lawless and without a king. After a time, the marvellous sword was forgotten except by a few who had kept their faith, sure that a miracle would eventually occur.

But now the time has come to meet Merlin, the magician, Archimedes, his pet owl and the other creatures who lived close to his cottage in the heart of a wood.

CHAPTER ONE ·

Deep in the heart of a vast forest stood a long, rambling cottage. Constructed of stone and blackened oak timbers, it had a thatched roof and a number of small, dusty windows. A cottage of secrets, it held a variety of fascinating treasures for Merlin, the sage and magician, lived there. In a glade close to the dwelling, a deep well supplied sparkling water, clear as crystal. Nearby, a stream murmured and sang as it wound its merry way through the flowers and foliage clustering along its banks. Overhead, tall trees met like giant umbrellas so that the sunlight filtered through in varying depths of green and gold.

The mysterious forest was alive with numerous inhabitants. Wood pigeons flew upwards in a cloud, birds with gleaming white-ringed necks, cooing and calling softly to one another. A variety of birds sang from their perches on the lofty trees, frogs croaked, crickets hopped in the lush grass and squirrels raced up and down tree trunks. An occasional pig rooted around an oak searching for acorns, its pink blotched body resembling a fat bolster. Wolves lurked in the shadows, green eyes glinting as they stalked their prey.

It was a warm September afternoon and the rich mellow ripeness of approaching autumn was in the air. Under the leafy shade of a tree a large grey wolf was crunching noisily on a bone. All around his feet lay a pile of smaller bones, already picked clean. The wolf's strong teeth bit into the marrow but even as he was chewing, his restless eyes were searching for signs of another tasty morsel. A cheeky red squirrel hopped boldly on to a limb just above the wolf's head, then dashed higher into the protective branches. Chattering noisily, he pulled a face at the wolf before seeking refuge inside a small hollow. Moments later, his impudent furry body appeared again on the tree limb. It wasn't only the wolf who was looking for an extra snack. A hawk was lurking in the vicinity, too. From his look-out his sharp eyes spied the red squirrel and swiftly he rose into the air, ready to strike. Sweeping forward, he dropped like a whirlwind. Just in time, the squirrel heard the whirr of powerful wings, ducked, and then, chattering with annoyance, he returned to the security of his hole in the tree trunk.

The cottage door opened and Merlin the magician stepped into a sunlit glade and crossed to the well. A sweeping purple cloak hung about him in heavy folds and he wore a tall violet-coloured hat which rose to a sharp point. Beneath the hat, fringes of frosty white hair poked out in rebellious tufts and a luxuriant silvery beard flowed down almost to his knees. The magician's shoes were long and very pointed.

He lowered the bucket into the well, then tugging on a heavy chain, began to haul it up. Shaking his head he muttered, 'It's a dark age indeed . . . an age of inconvenience. No plumbing, no electricity, in fact, no nothing!' As the bucket came to the surface the lower part of Merlin's beard floated in the water. Impatiently, he shook the glistening drops away and then, hearing a sound in the forest, looked round. 'Oh, now what? Now what?' he said testily. Unable to discern anything unusual he turned away from the well clutching his pail of water. The toe of his long shoe caught in the chain, almost tripping him. Glaring, he cursed, 'You . . . you fiendish chain, you.' Stepping over the chain, he re-entered the cottage.

Although wise in many ways, the magician acted at times in an absent-minded fashion. Now and again he did silly things, for his mind, seldom on everyday living, was bound up in higher realms of thought. He possessed the amazing power of being able to see way back into the murky past and centuries ahead into the dim and distant future. It was an awe-inspiring gift and as he lived constantly

13

in a three-dimensional world he seldom bothered to keep his mind focused on the immediate present. The past, and more especially the future, were much more interesting.

The cottage door creaked as the magician pushed it wide and entered the living room. Using his left foot he slammed the door shut and walked over to the stove. 'Everything's so complicated,' he continued to mutter, 'just one big medieval mess.'

A handsome owl with golden brown feathers, a thick silvery ruff and large tawny eyes surveyed Merlin placidly from his perch. The owl, known as Archimedes, lived with the magician and was his constant companion. Instead of nesting in a tree, he had a house of his own inside the cottage, an arrangement which suited him very well. Used to his master's mutterings he seldom took them seriously. He flew inside his own little house while Merlin poured water into the tea-kettle.

The main room of the cottage was dominated by a large fireplace and, immediately above, a large hole in the roof showed glimpses of blue sky and the lacy pattern of trees. A hook was suspended from an iron bar above the fireplace from which Merlin hung his cooking pots. The centre of the room was occupied by a square wooden table and a few chairs. Along the back wall a bunk bed was concealed behind wooden shutters. Benches ran round two of the walls and their surfaces were littered with an assortment of strange objects and many sheets of parchment covered with fine writing. The fourth wall served as a bookcase and contained hundreds of volumes.

Having filled the tea-kettle, Merlin removed his tall, pointed hat, wiped the damp fringes of his hair then resettled his hat back on his head. Taking a magic watch from his pocket he stared at it thoughtfully.

'Now . . . let me see. Ummm . . . he should be here in . . . ah . . . I'd say half . . . yes, half an hour.'

Looking puzzled, Archimedes backed carefully out of his tiny house on to a branch. 'Who? Who?' he hooted. 'I'd like to know who?'

Merlin replaced his watch and, crossing the room, pulled out a chair. Picking up his magic cane, he pointed to the hole in the roof. 'I told you, Archimedes, I am not sure. All I know is that someone will be coming. Someone very important!'

Archimedes stared at his master with wide, unblinking eyes. Nodding his head, the magician proceeded to measure the distance from the chair to the ceiling. 'Ah . . . Fate will direct him to me so that I in turn may guide him to his rightful place in the world.'

Archimedes flapped his wings then flew from his perch. 'Hah! And you say he will arrive in half an hour?' Circling the room twice, he returned to his perch. 'Hah! Well, we'll just see.'

Merlin smiled as he sat down and lit his pipe. The match burned his finger and he dropped it on the floor before starting to blow smoke rings into the air. 'And you will, Archimedes, you will. He'll be a boy . . . a small boy. Eleven, possibly twelve years old, and a scrawny little fellow.' The smoke rings had changed into a dense bluish cloud and Merlin gazed up at its varying formations. In the centre of the cloud a tall young man with a mop of brown hair and broad shoulders was walking rapidly. He reached a wall, leapt over it and disappeared. Merlin frowned. 'Oh, no, no, no! That can't be the one. Surely not! Why . . . that big lad must be closer to twenty.' He stared into the smoke cloud again. A much smaller boy with hair the colour of a wheatfield suddenly appeared and climbed the wall, too. 'There . . . there he is!' muttered Merlin, satisfaction in his voice. 'Ha, ha, ha. A scrawny little fellow about twelve. A regular little grasshopper.' The magician leaned back and rubbed his nose, laughing with glee.

'Heh, look at him go!' The yellow-haired boy ran along the top of the wall and then leapt off.

'And where would you guess he is at this very moment?' enquired Archimedes, still flapping about on his perch.

Merlin turned to answer and banged himself on the arm of the chair. He pulled a face at his absent-mindedness for he was always forgetting about the arms. 'I am not guessing, Archimedes . . . I know where he is! Ah . . . less than a mile from here just beyond the forest.' Merlin glanced again into the smoky cloud which, for him alone, revealed many secrets. The two boys were now scrambling up a hill. The younger one clambered on to a dead tree branch. Merlin could see them clearly and he nodded his satisfaction. 'Yes . . . and right on schedule if all goes well.' Leaning back in his chair he puffed deeply on his pipe. He had only to wait.

Meanwhile, a little over a mile away two boys were playing, just as the magician had spied in the smoke. They raced up a gentle slope of a hill and when they reached its summit, paused to scan the horizon. The bigger of the two boys, who was known as Kay, carried a bow and arrows. A mud track rose steeply to a hillside farm. Barns gleamed golden with cut hay, the sweet fragrance scenting the air. The fields were covered with yellow stubble, the aftermath of recent scything. Rabbits leapt in and out of hedgerows, merging with late-afternoon shadows. A fox suddenly appeared from behind a barn, his red coat glistening in the sun, his bushy tail white-tipped. But the two eager boys were not

observing the tranquil countryside; rather they were gazing with absorbed interest towards the forest, strangely remote and mysterious.

Kay hissed in the younger one's ear, 'Quiet, Wart!'

Wart, from his position on the dead branch whispered, 'Ah . . . I'm trying to be.'

Kay sniffed. 'Nobody asked you to come along in the first place.' Kay could be an ungracious lad.

'I'm not even moving,' said Wart defensively.

A smile lit up Kay's sullen features. For a moment he looked pleased. 'Shut up! Here we go.'

Wart followed the direction of Kay's glance. From the mossy green shadows of the wood a handsome young deer had appeared. The creature sniffed the air delicately before moving daintily into a small glade. 'Oh . . . what a set up,' said Kay, his voice tinged with excitement. Taking an arrow from its quiver he set it in the bow, taking careful aim. The arrow quivered with tension as he drew it back. Wart's blue eyes widened in disapproval. 'Right smack through the old gizzard,' murmured Kay rather vulgarly.

In that instant the deer looked up, a second sense alerting it to imminent danger. At that same moment the dead branch on which Wart was kneeling gave way with a loud snap and it fell

earthwards bringing the young boy down with it . . . right on to Kay's head. The arrow misfired, going off at a tangent and disappearing inside the forest. The deer, swift as the wind, was already vanishing amongst an avenue of trees.

Kay turned on the younger boy in hot anger. 'Little fool,' he yelled, chasing and trying to strike Wart with his bow.

'Gosh, Kay . . . I'm sorry. I couldn't help it.'

Kay was not in a forgiving mood. 'If I ever get my hands on you, I'll . . . ouch!' He tripped over a log, falling heavily to the ground. Jumping up immediately, not bothering to brush the dust and leaves from his breeches, he dashed in pursuit of Wart. 'I'll wring your scrawny little neck, so help me I will.'

Wart, secretly pleased that the deer had escaped an unfortunate end, peered from behind a tree trunk. 'I'll get the arrow, Kay. I'm sure I can find it.'

Kay looked in mockery at the tow-headed, eager eyed boy. Sarcastically, he pointed into the mysterious green depths of the forest. 'Oh, don't tell me you're going in there? Ah, ha, ha, ha. Why, it's swarming with wolves.'

Wart drew himself up to his full height, even though that didn't amount to very much. 'I'm not afraid,' he retorted boldly.

Kay shrugged. 'Well, go ahead. It's your skin, not mine.' Indifferent to the fate of his young companion, he turned his back on the tall whispering trees and the small boy and walked back in the direction from which he had come.

Left to his own devices, Wart paused, then climbed on to a boulder to take a look around. His bright red jerkin and long golden brown stockings made a brilliant splash of colour against the soft mellow hues of the trees. There was no sign of the arrow - he would have to go deeper into the forest. He spotted an old, overgrown path leading into the forest, that seemed to hint at mystery and excitement. A group of jays called noisily, tearing at the waiting silence. Wart jumped from the boulder and started to walk along the forest path. A lean grey wolf slunk from behind rocks where, seconds earlier, Wart had been peering about him. The boy hurried on, looking first at the ground, then up at the tall trees forming a canopy and blotting out the sun's brilliance. It was eerie and dark and Wart felt very much alone.

Suddenly he fell over a stout branch lying across the path. Telling himself that he should look where he was going, he seized the low-lying branch of an overhanging tree and tried valiantly to bend it down to the ground. He almost succeeded, then having tested his skill, swiftly let it go. The move was lucky for him. Stalking close behind was a lean, grey wolf and, as the ever-hungry creature popped its head out from a clump of bushes ready to seize the boy, the branch struck the wolf a resounding blow. With a sharp yelp he ran off into the underbrush. Wart looked round with a startled expression and hurried on, his heart hammering.

Moving quickly and quietly through the trees he smiled happily when he spotted the missing arrow, buried deep in the trunk of a sturdy oak. Dashing forward with a joyous whoop of triumph, Wart started to climb the massive gnarled trunk. Only just in time! The determined wolf had recovered from the blow he had received and was back on the trail. As the boy scrambled upwards, the wolf snapped viciously at his heels. Thoroughly alarmed, Wart moved higher. Below, the wolf snarled, baring its long fangs. Wart looked down with a tremor. The wolf's mouth was open as it loped round the base of the tree. It looked particularly vicious.

A slight breeze suddenly freshened, rustling the leaves so that they whispered and fans of sunlight slanted through the moving branches. Wart looked

round at the leaves, stepped on to a limb without caution . . . and it broke. Frantically he grabbed at another branch and clung with desperation. The wolf leered up at him. The tree limb fell right into the wolf's open mouth. With an angry shake of the head, the wolf spat the limb out and pawed the ground. He was becoming impatient as he waited for the tempting morsel dangling provocatively above him to drop down like a plum. For the wolf it would be easy pickings. Optimistically, he opened his mouth again.

But Wart was destined for greater things than making a tasty meal for a greedy wolf. Merlin's cottage, like an agent of fate, lay hidden by trees just beyond the giant oak where young Wart was virtually a prisoner. Recklessly, he reached for the embedded arrow . . . missed . . . and fell, crashing through the branches and right through the hole in Merlin's roof.

The magician's prediction had come true!

CHAPTER TWO

A mighty whooshing sound filled Wart's ears and before he had time to realise what was happening, he landed with a heavy thump on the floor of the cottage. A shower of twigs and other debris descended with him. Gingerly, he picked himself up, brushing a cobweb from his red jerkin. Merlin, still seated in a chair close to the table, raised his hands and brushed away a cloud of dust. He looked with keen interest at his visitor, who appeared to have descended from the heavens.

'So . . .' he said with an amused smile, '. . . you did drop in for tea after all.'

Bewildered, Wart looked around the unusual room, quite speechless for the moment. Merlin pulled his watch from the folds of a voluminous gown he wore beneath his purple cloak. 'Hmmmm . . . you are a bit late, you know!'

Wart could only stare in dumbfounded fashion at the cottage, its weird contents and even more curious owner. To give the boy time to collect himself, Merlin crossed to the stove and poured water into the tea-kettle from the pot. He gestured to a chair, indicating that Wart could sit down if he chose. The boy dropped into a chair close to the table.

Merlin cleared his throat. 'Now, my name is Merlin. Come, come, tell me lad, who are you?'

Wart stared frankly at the magician. 'Oh, my name's Arthur but everyone calls me Wart.'

Merlin raised expressive eyebrows at the nickname but made no comment. Lifting the lid of

23

the teapot he peered inside. Archimedes sat motionless on his perch and the boy and the bird stared unblinkingly at each other. 'Oh,' said Wart with enthusiasm, 'what a perfect stuffed owl.'

. Archimedes spluttered with indignation and ruffled his feathers before taking off from his perch and flying several times round the room. 'Stuffed bird indeed!' he squawked.

'Gosh . . . he's alive and he talks,' said Wart in wonderment.

'Oh yes . . . and a great deal better than you do,' replied the owl huffily.

Merlin poured tea. 'Come now, Archimedes. Come now. I want you to meet Wart. You must forgive him, he's only a young boy!'

'Boy? Boy?' screeched the owl. 'I see no boy.' Deliberately he closed his eyes.

Merlin pushed a cup of tea across the table towards Wart and placed an arm about his slim shoulders. 'I . . . I'm sorry that I called him a stuffed . . .' began Wart.

'That's all right. Heh, heh, heh! He's much too sensitive, our dear Archimedes.'

The owl dropped on to its perch, ran along its length and squeezed through into his private domain, noisily banging the door. On the inside, safe from prying eyes, he leant against it and listened intently to the conversation.

Wart took a sip of tea. It tasted good so he took another sip. 'How did you know I was . . .'

'Oh, that! That you'd be dropping in?' interrupted Merlin. The magician picked up his own cup, slopping some of the amber liquid down his silver beard. He shook away the drops of moisture. 'Ha, ha. Well . . . I happen to be a wizard. A soothsayer. Yes,' continued Merlin, 'I'm a prognosticator.' Wart's eyes opened wide at the long words. Merlin took off the glasses he often wore and held them up to the light. 'I have the power to see into the future. *Centuries* into the future!' With an extravagant gesture he indicated the cluttered benches running round two walls of the room. 'I've been there, lad, and I've seen all these things.'

Wart's eyes grew as big as saucers in his small face as he listened in fascination, while his gaze rested on objects that to him were unrecognisable; models of trains, aeroplanes, ships, space-craft and all manner of modern inventions.

Merlin smiled, understanding his guest's wonderment. 'Of course, they're only plans and small models.' From the bench he picked up a locomotive, bringing it over to the table for Wart's closer observation. 'Ha, ha . . . now take this for instance. It's a steam locomotive.' Pouring hot water from the kettle into a hole in the model engine, he stopped the boiler with a cork and gave the model a shove. The locomotive steamed across the table. 'There she goes,' commented Merlin in satisfaction. 'Ha, ha. Pretty good, eh?'

Wart held his breath in admiration and as the engine drew level with him he turned it round so that it chugged merrily on its way. Merlin locked his hands together and watched as interestedly as his young observer. 'That won't be invented for hundreds and hundreds of years.'

Wart looked shocked. 'Oh, . . . do you mean you can see everything before it happens?'

Merlin picked up the little puffing engine. 'Yes . . . everything!'

Archimedes hastily opened the door of his tiny house and eased into sight. Solemnly he shook his head, staring unflinchingly at the magician. 'Everything, Merlin?' he asked.

Merlin met the owl's bright stare. 'Well, no. Not *everything*. Nearly everything! I admit I didn't know whom to expect for tea . . . not exactly . . . and yet I figured the exact place.' Picking up his cane he pointed to the hole in the roof where Wart had come crashing through.

Wart nodded. 'You're very clever, sir.' Merlin lowered the cane, accidentally hitting Wart on the head with it.

Ruefully the little boy rubbed the top of his head where already a small bump was starting to form. The wizard was inclined to be absent-minded. 'Yes . . . well, never mind the sir. Plain Merlin will do,' said the magician. Deciding to show his visitor some further magic he offered him more tea. Wart accepted. 'Now, would you care for sugar,' enquired Merlin.

Wart nodded and Merlin clapped his hands together. The sugar bowl picked up a spoon and danced across the table to Merlin's cup. 'No, No! Manners, manners,' snapped the magician in reprimanding tones. 'Guests first, you know that.' The sugar bowl flipped its lid into the air by way of an apology, then marched across the table to Wart. 'All right, say when, lad.' Merlin smiled at the boy's astonishment.

'When!' whispered Wart to the obliging sugar bowl as it spooned sugar generously into his cup. Shyly, he helped himself to cake while Merlin crossed to the bookshelf and selected an impressive looking volume. 'Have you had any schooling?' the magician enquired.

Hastily swallowing a mouthful of cake, Wart nodded. 'Oh yes! I'm training to be a squire. I'm learning the rules of combat and swordmanship and jousting and horsemanship.'

Merlin picked up the teapot. In anticipation, the sugar bowl hastily rushed across the table spooning sugar into the magician's cup. Merlin nodded his thanks and turned again to Wart. 'Good . . . yes, that's very good. But I mean *real* education. Mathematics, history, biology, natural history, science, English, Latin, French . . .' He broke off in sudden annoyance when he noticed that the over obliging sugar bowl had filled his cup to the brim with sugar. 'No, no . . . blast it all,' he scolded.

Shaking his fist he said loudly, *'When!'* It was the sugar bowl's signal to stop and indeed, there wasn't room for any more in the cup. Cramming its lid on its dish it took refuge behind the large teapot. With a show of exasperation, Merlin emptied the sugar from his cup on to the table, then swept it to the floor with his beard.

The magician set a pile of books on to the table with a loud thump and wiggled his finger at a chair which obligingly moved towards him. With a giant sigh the wizard sat down. 'Impudent piece of crockery,' he muttered with a scowl, glancing at the mischievous bowl which was still trying to hide. The magician's penetrating eyes studied Wart. 'You can't grow up without a decent education, you know!' Selecting one of the books he opened it and announced, 'So I am going to be your tutor!'

Wart was stunned. Rising, he helped himself to another slice of cake and looked towards the cottage door. 'But I've gotta get back to the castle. They'll want me in the kitchen.' His voice carried a note of alarm.

As if anticipating an argument, Merlin reached for a holdall. Setting it in the middle of the floor, he opened it. 'Oh, well then . . . very well . . . we'll pack and be on our way.' He chuckled.

Archimedes had pricked up his ears at Merlin's words and he ran along his perch calling softly, 'Whoo whoo . . . Whoo whoo . . . '

Wart hesitated by the cottage door, poised for flight. It was growing late and he knew that he would be in for trouble when he finally did arrive back at the castle. Sir Ector, his guardian and foster-father, could show his anger in a number of ways and it usually led to Wart finding himself with an impossible amount of extra chores to carry out.

Merlin, however, was determined to tutor his little guest whether he liked it or not, so he prepared to put his magic in motion. 'You . . . you watch now. You'll like this,' he told Wart. Despite doubts, the fascinated boy couldn't tear his gaze away from the magician. Merlin raised his cane with the intention of striking the stool in front of him. Unfortunately the cane became tangled in his long beard and that took a few moments to sort out. Starting again, the magician raised his arms high above his head. 'I want your attention everything,' he called staring round the cottage at the varied contents. The utensils on the table turned in the direction of the speaker, the furniture leaned slightly forward, even the books appeared to be listening. Wart, thoroughly captivated, came back inside the cottage and sat at the table. He couldn't miss such an incredible feat of magic. Just wait till he got back to the castle and told Kay about it, he thought. He'd wish that he too, had ventured into the mysterious forest.

'We're packing to leave,' explained Merlin to the room in general. 'Come on, let's go! No . . . no, no, no . . . not you,' he warned the sugar bowl as it made a move. 'Books are always the first, you know. Shrink in size!' commanded Merlin. 'Very small, we've got to save enough room for all.'

Archimedes fluttered from his perch and sat on the volumes still on the table. The sugar bowl peeked out cheekily from its hiding place behind the enormous teapot, then boldly marched towards Merlin. All the books from the shelves, now diminished in size, strutted towards the holdall. The owl almost slipped as the volumes beneath him moved to join their companions in the procession. Wart picked up the sugar bowl's spoon and cover but, suddenly aware that something was missing, the sugar bowl hastily returned, snatching the items from Wart's hand. The little boy couldn't repress his laughter.

Further amusement was to follow. The teapot and other dishes, jars of jam, cutlery and bits of bric-à-brac all formed a queue. It was rather disorderly, for the mischief-making sugar bowl was intent on stirring up trouble as well as tea. Aggressively it picked a fight with the teapot hitting it viciously with its spoon. There was an ominous crack. The line stopped and there was a pile-up as the different items all fell over each other. General confusion reigned.

Merlin frowned, tugged his beard and waved his arms in the air. Knocking books from out of his path, he moved over to the sugar bowl, still engaged in its fierce battle with the luckless teapot. 'See here, sugar bowl,' he said crossly, 'You're getting too rough. That poor old tea-set is cracked enough. Now take it easy. All right . . . all right!' He gazed up and down the disorderly line. 'Let's start again!' Exasperated, he ran his cane through his hair, accidentally knocking his tall wizard's hat sideways. 'Oh . . . where was I, boy?' He turned to Wart with a lost expression on his face.

When he had recovered his good humour, Merlin sat on a stool ready to resume his magic. Looking disgustedly at the surrounding chaos, Archimedes flew round the room three times and then, in a huff, shut himself up in his little house. Merlin muttered an incantation and waved his magic cane. It had an immediate effect. A globe of the world, test-tubes, models, furniture and rugs sailed through the air, growing smaller and smaller as they travelled towards the holdall. Even Wart's chair suddenly rose from the ground. With lightning agility he leapt off. He didn't wish to grow very tiny, like the other things in the room.

Wart's eyes opened wide in sudden horror. The owl's house was shrinking to a dimunitive size. Whatever would happen to the bird? The door flew open and with tawny eyes flashing fury, Archimedes managed to crawl out . . . just in time. 'Bungling blockhead!' he hooted rudely to Merlin.

The magician merely smiled. He was used to the owl's tantrums. Sliding to the floor he muttered, 'What a way to pack!' The case snapped itself shut as it was now full to the brim. The job was done and Wart shook his head in amazement. What he had just witnessed was a miracle. 'It's hard to believe,' the boy whispered confidentially to the magician.

'Yes . . . but just a minute, lad. How else would you get all this stuff into one suitcase, I'd like to know?' To Merlin it was obvious that miracles were an everyday occurrence and not something to be wondered at. From a rafter, Archimedes sniffed at the magician's words. He was still feeling angry at the idea of being sandwiched into the overfull holdall.

'Oh, I think it's wonderful . . . in fact I think that you're wonderful,' blurted out Wart, filled with admiration for his new-found friend.

Merlin lifted the case as though it weighed no more than a handful of feathers, crossed to the front door and placed it in the clearing. Returning, he picked up his magic cane and, as Wart prepared to follow him from the cottage, the magician said suddenly, 'Now wait! Don't get any foolish ideas that magic will solve all your problems.'

'Oh, no . . . no, sir!'

'Because it won't,' said Merlin warningly. He didn't want the lad to think that magic formulas could transform life into a comfortable bed of roses. That wouldn't do at all.

'But sir, I don't have any problems,' insisted Wart, who at that particular moment was convinced that he hadn't.

Man and boy walked out into the clearing, into the late autumn afternoon laced with lengthening green shadows and slender rays of mellow sunshine. 'Oh, pah! Everybody's got problems . . . the world is full of problems!' Merlin turned to close the cottage door. 'Whoo . . . whoo . . .' A cry of indignation rent the air and with a loud swishing of wings, Archimedes descended hastily from his perch in the rafters and fluttered into the open. He looked furious. Living with the brilliant but absent-minded magician was like walking a tightrope. If he saw you were there, fine! If he were lost in his dreams, look out! Merlin, preoccupied with other matters seemed unaware of the owl's near imprisonment inside the lonely, deserted cottage. Disgruntled, Archimedes ruffled his feathers.

The magician's beard caught in the door. 'Oh, blast it all!' he exploded, twisting round in an effort to extricate it. His erratic movement only succeeded in wrapping the beard more firmly about his throat like a long silver scarf. Merlin finally straightened out the tangle with the aid of his cane. At last, he closed the cottage with a resounding bang and turned the key in the lock. 'There now . . . you see what I mean,' he ranted, picking up the suitcase.

Wart stifled a giggle as he and Merlin stepped on to the mossy path leading through the forest. At last, they were ready to start on their journey to the castle.

3

CHAPTER THREE

Archimedes stretched his wings and flew on to the top of Merlin's tall cap. The perch was comfortable and he could listen to the conversation. As the trio commenced their journey, a grey wolf who had been slinking amongst the trees thrust his head into the open, licking his chops. It was the same wolf who had followed Wart earlier in the afternoon, before the boy had fallen through the hole in Merlin's roof. As Wart strode out jauntily beside the magician, the wolf eyed him hungrily. He considered that the boy would make a tasty snack. Cautiously, the crafty animal began to slink along at a discreet distance.

Walking deeper along the forest trail, the air took on a dusky bluish tinge resembling the interior of a cavern. Wart shivered nervously, glad of company. Beside the constantly murmuring stream a dazzle of orange marigolds shone brightly, an unexpected and welcome illumination; birds sang in the dense foliage, occasionally swooping low across the path in their quest for tiny insects. Two butterflies, quivering gold and purple shapes, alighted momentarily on a leaf. The forest held a magnetic quality all its own. Wart was happy to let his enquiring gaze rove in various directions.

'You see . . . that's the trouble with the world

today,' Merlin was saying. 'Everybody butting their heads against a brick wall. All muscle and no mentality.' He glanced down at his small companion. 'Do *you* want to be all muscle and no brain?' Stopping in his tracks he gazed fixedly at Wart's earnest face.

Wart stuck out his lower lip reflectively. 'I don't have any muscle!' He glanced at his thin arms showing below the short sleeves of his red jerkin. Further back along the trail, the sly wolf stopped his stealthy padding, too. He had no wish to be spotted.

'Ah . . . you don't have any muscle?' asked Merlin. 'Then how do you move about?'

Wart examined his arm again flexing the muscles so that they made a small bulge. 'I suppose I do have a little,' he admitted.

'Ah hah . . . there, you see?' The magician turned in the direction of a gully, carelessly swinging the holdall. 'Well, that's enough! Now develop your *brain*!'

Wart remained stationary, pondering on the wise man's words. All the time the artful wolf was creeping closer and closer on velvet-padded paws. Almost level, he opened his wide hungry jaws to take a savage bite from Wart's leg. Still unaware of the wolf's presence, the boy moved in Merlin's direction . . . in the nick of time!

The magician was balancing on a tree stump. He leapt across the gully and Wart prepared to follow. 'Knowledge, wisdom . . . there's the real power,' he said to his little charge, as he landed on the opposite bank and scrambled up the slope. 'Higher learning - yes, that's the thing!'

The wolf was determined not to be outdone. Attempting to jump across the gully, he slipped, and was left dangling precariously from a tree stump. His calamity was his own. He remained unnoticed as the trio moved on.

Merlin strode along a ridge. 'So my lad, first

thing tomorrow morning we start a full schedule.' The magician's foot slipped and he slid down the slope right into the water, Archimedes still perched on his hat. The bird squawked but, unperturbed, Merlin climbed on to the bank again, still talking. 'Yes! Eight hours a day. We'll have six hours for the school room, and two for study period.'

The ground was damp and slippery and, pretty soon, Wart too had followed suit and taken a ducking. Damp and mud-stained he plodded along after Merlin. 'But I don't have the time for studying,' he tried to explain. 'I have my page duties.'

'Page duties? Pah!' Merlin was disgusted. 'Page duties indeed!' In the magician's eyes they were stuff and nonsense, a waste of time.

Wart slid back into the water, caught off balance by the wizard's disgust. For a moment he sat in the shallows but, since Merlin continued walking, the boy got to his feet again and ran to catch up. He didn't wish to be left too far behind in the forest. It was eerie and rather frightening.

On the opposite side of the gully, the wolf was in a predicament. He couldn't continue clinging for much longer to the tree stump and yet if he should let go . . . ? Glaring down fearfully at the rushing waters below, his green eyes flashed fire. What could he do? Whimpering, he closed his eyes and let go. None too gently, he hit the slope, sliding swiftly towards the water. Frantically, he dug his claws into the damp earth but it was no use. Splash! With a shiver as the waters closed over his head he sank down . . . down . . . down even lower, bumping himself on a submerged rock. At long last, after a great struggle, he surfaced and struck out grimly for the shore, growling and cursing as he swam.

Merlin had gained the top of the hill and was leaping easily over a pile of rocks. Wart, slightly out of breath, managed to catch up with him at last. Just then, a shower of boulders and shale broke loose and started rolling down the hillside with a loud grinding sound, gathering speed as it travelled. The avalanche missed the band of travellers who, engrossed in Merlin's words, never even noticed it. But the luckless wolf below wasn't quite so fortunate!

The magician turned to the boy at his side. 'Referring to those page duties, we will have to change all that. There's got to be a shake-up.' Wart nodded, feeling it was a good idea to agree although he felt sure that his guardian would never give his consent. Merlin went on talking, pressing home his point. 'How do you ever expect to amount to anything without an education, I'd like to know? Even in these bungling, backward, medieval times you've got to know where you're going, haven't you?'

Wart was swift to acknowledge this wisdom. 'Yes . . . ah, yes!'

'You must plan for the future, boy. You've got to find a direction.' Putting the holdall on the ground, Merlin looked around him, saying, 'Now, by the by, in what direction is this castle of yours?'

Wart pointed in the opposite direction saying meekly, 'Well, sir . . . I think it's north . . . the other way!'

Archimedes shrugged. Still perched on top of Merlin's hat his attitude indicated that that was just what he would have expected. All this time and they had been walking the wrong way! The magician rolled his eyes. 'Oh! All right, then. We'd better get a move on. Come on, come on, lad.' He veered sharply left, causing the owl to lose his balance. Angrily, the bird fluttered into the air before resettling with a forcible thud.

As Merlin and Wart slid down the hill again they passed within yards of the wolf struggling grimly towards the top. His tongue was hanging out, his breath coming in short gasps. One of the loose boulders had struck him a glancing blow, another even larger one had narrowly missed him. He was in a foul temper. He sat down miserably, watching his intended supper snack recrossing the gully accompanied by the magician . . . and getting further and further away with every passing second. It was too much! Concluding that it just wasn't his day, the wolf slunk off into a clump of trees growling throatily. He'd remember that whippersnapper of a boy! He vowed that he would!

Blissfully unaware of the danger that had menaced him from the very second he left the wizard's cottage, Wart hurried to keep pace with his companion. The sun-mellowed afternoon had given way to evening and a flamboyant saffron, green and crimson sunset hung in splendid bars across the sky as the sun, a great coppery ball, slid lower on the horizon. Soon twilight lay across the land, as early stars blinked sleepily against the approaching canopy of night. The forest was now far behind the travellers, a vast dim shadowy quilt. The open fields assumed a darker, closed-in look. The warm fragrant air began to cool and a breeze stirred the hedgerows.

Wart began to feel tired. It was a long walk and he'd had a strange and exciting day. Glancing up at Merlin, now not much more than a vague shadow in the soft light, he wondered about how their reception would go when they finally did reach the castle. Sir Ector, his guardian, might well be very angry. He was a touchy man and Wart had learned to respect his moods.

Merlin pointed to a distant light shining like a beacon across the countryside. 'Is that it, boy?'

'Yes . . . yes, sir, that's it.'

'And about time,' grumbled the magician.

'Yes . . . about time,' echoed Archimedes from his perch.

Inside the castle, Ector was pacing back and forth in the vast main hall, his face flushed and angry. The walls were hung with an assortment of weapons, whilst suits of armour graced a number of deep niches. Close to a log fire a large dog lolled, his tongue hanging out as he stared at the fitful flames. Kay, Ector's son, was seated at a long refectory table occupying the central part of the hall. His feet rested on the table's edge as he munched noisily on a juicy turkey leg. Sir Ector paused in his pacing and leant against a timbered doorway. 'Devil take it, anyone's got better sense than to go bargin' off into that infernal forest alone. You'd no business letting him go,' he ranted, scowling at his son.

Kay was unperturbed. 'Look, dad. I'm not Wart's keeper.' He flung a bone towards the fireplace and it was immediately snapped up by the large dog.

'Well, blast it all, I am.' Ector was vexed. Flinging himself into a seat he mopped his forehead with a square of linen. 'After all, I took him in, adopted the lad you might say and, being his foster-father, well . . . I'm responsible.'

From another part of the castle several dogs barked in unison. Seconds later three of the animals charged into the hall, dashing madly towards the front door. Wart entered and was bowled to the ground by his doggie reception committee, jumping over him with ecstatic greetings, licking his face and hands and tugging playfully at his clothes. Merlin, unannounced and so far unnoticed, stood on the threshold watching the scene, Archimedes still sitting on his hat.

Ector clapped his hands and issued a sharp command to the excited dogs. Looking sheepish, they backed away from Wart. 'What's the big idea gallivantin' off in the woods and worrying the living daylights out of everybody?' Sir Ector fixed the boy with a stern, questioning countenance.

Wart looked crestfallen. He'd expected trouble and here it was. 'I . . . I'm sorry, sir.'

Ector raised four fingers in the air. 'Well, sorry's not enough. That's four demerits. Four hours extra kitchen duty. Report to the cook . . . at once!'

Wart, still seated on the flagstones where the dogs had bowled him over looked unhappy. 'But sir, I'd like to . . .'

The knight was in no mood to listen. He clapped his hands again. 'Hop to it, boy. Off to the kitchens. Yes . . . you've gotta keep a tight schedule to run a big place like this.'

Clambering tiredly to his feet, Wart hurried across to a cellar and disappeared inside its gloomy interior. Sir Ector nodded his satisfaction and looked at Kay. 'Discipline . . . yes, we need strict rules, especially for small boys.'

'And I most certainly agree!' The unexpected retort came from Archimedes who was growing impatient, sitting unnoticed in the background. He wasn't used to being ignored.

Sir Ector spun round, surprise registered on his red face. 'And who are you?'

Merlin poked Archimedes with his cane. Resentfully, the owl flapped off his hat and round the hall, finally perching on a mounted deer's head. From a spiky antler he glared down at the upturned faces. Merlin stepped forward. 'Let me introduce myself. I am Merlin . . . and this,' he said, pointing to the irritated bird, 'is Archimedes, a highly educated owl.'

The knight was visibly shaken. 'An educated owl, did you say? Oh ho . . . that's a good one! Say, you must have him under a spell, Marvin. You're a magician, huh?'

Merlin drew himself up to his full height. 'The name is *Merlin* and I happen to be the world's most powerful wizard.'

Sir Ector blinked first in disbelief then started to laugh, exclaiming, 'Gadzooks . . . a wizard indeed!'

Merlin did not appreciate being laughed at - especially by strangers. 'Very well,' he replied. 'I shall demonstrate.' Waving his cane he murmured, 'Wind and snow . . . swirl and blow.'

Within seconds, a dense mass of snowflakes danced and cavorted into the heated hall before a strong, icy wind. 'Brrr . . .' said Sir Ector, starting to shiver as small snowdrifts piled up around his feet and a white mantle of crisp flakes built up on his shoulders. Hugging himself to keep warm he stared at the magician in frank astonishment.

Looking amused, Merlin tugged on his long silver beard. 'And that is what I call a wizard blizzard.'

Sir Ector looked at Kay who, though shivering, was still eating. 'Hey, Kay, would you look at this? An indoor blizzard in summer weather. Who'd have believed it!' He turned to Merlin. 'All right, Marvin. Turn her off . . . I'm convinced.'

Satisfied, the magician raised his arms. The wind ceased as suddenly as it had begun and the last of the snowflakes drifted lazily to the floor and started to melt. Ector shook snow from his hair and brushed it off his jacket. 'I hope you don't go in for any of that *black* magic,' he said glancing worriedly at Merlin.

The wizard shook his head. 'Oh . . . no, no, no! Never touch the stuff. My magic is used mainly for ah . . . educational purposes.' He gestured towards his holdall just inside the doorway. 'In fact, that is why I am here. I have come to educate Wart.'

Ector was not pleased. He walked aggressively over to Merlin, shouting, 'Oh, no you don't! I'm running this place. If you think you're going to fiddle with my schedule, you'd better pack up your bag of tricks and be gone!' He stamped his foot. A second later he blinked, not sure if he could believe his eyes. 'Kay . . . Kay,' he called, 'he's *gone*!'

Kay blew snowflakes off another turkey leg and bit into it. 'Good riddance,' he said with his mouth full.

A voice came from the ether. 'I'm gone . . . but then I'm not gone.'

Puzzled, Ector looked round the hall, examined the niches where the suits of armour stood, then opened the suitcase. There was no sign of Merlin and yet . . . Ector knew he'd just heard his voice.

'So if I do leave,' continued the invisible magician, 'You can never be sure that I'm really gone, can you?'

'Well, I must say, you've got me there, Marvin. Yes . . . yes, you win!' Ector sighed. 'You're welcome to stay if you like.'

Merlin instantly reappeared, smiling pleasantly. 'You're very kind, very generous I must say.'

Ector patted the magician's back. 'Well, ah, all we can offer is room and board. Ah . . . hard times, you know . . .' He walked towards one of the doorways leading from the main hall, beckoning

Merlin to follow. 'We'll put you up in the north-west tower. Er . . . that's the guest room. It's a bit draughty in the winter but in this blazin' hot weather it's the best room in the house.'

Picking up the holdall, Merlin followed his host up a flight of narrow stone stairs leading to a rickety old tower. It was not at all prepossessing but it would have to do. At least, Merlin was inside the castle by invitation. 'Oh yes, very nice, very nice indeed,' he murmured politely.

Archimedes flew into the room with a loud whirring and flapping of wings. Ector looked at the owl in disapproval before turning again to Merlin. 'So just make yourself at home, Marvin.' After a swift glare at the bird and a cursory nod to Merlin, the knight turned on his heel and went swiftly down the uneven stairs, muttering under his breath.

'Marvin . . . Marvin . . . he will call me Marvin,' complained the wizard, opening his holdall and starting to unpack.

CHAPTER FOUR

By the following day the weather had changed. Dark, angry looking clouds scudded across the sky and a high wind scattered leaves from the trees. By late afternoon an ominous rumble of thunder was heard, followed by brilliant lightning flashes. Heavy rain soaked into the thirsty ground and also fell through the holes in the roof of the tower where Merlin and Archimedes had their quarters. Within a quarter of an hour, little streams were forming all over the floor. Exasperated by Sir Ector's ungracious hospitality, Merlin placed umbrellas close to the ceiling where the leaks were worst and, grabbing buckets and pails, stood them at strategic points in an effort to catch the drips.

'Best room in the house! Ha!' muttered the magician, as rain fell on the tip of his nose and splashed down onto his beard. 'Guest room . . . *unwelcome* guest room. But if he thinks he can get rid of me, I've got news for that old walrus. I'm sticking it out!'

Archimedes had taken refuge from the rain in his own little bird house. At least that didn't have a leaky roof. He stuck out his head to exclaim, 'And I say we go back to our cottage in the woods.'

Merlin picked up the cheeky sugar bowl, removed its lid and placed it on top of a stack of books to catch more drips. 'Oh, not on your life! That boy's got to have an education. He has a future.' Sugar bowl baled water out with his spoon then defiantly clamped the lid back on. He didn't want to be used as a water container. Besides, it would make his sugar awfully sticky.

The owl hooted. 'Ah, well, Merlin you may be right. A skinny kid like that would make a crackin' good chimney sweep.'

Smiling at the owl's rude remark the wizard pointed his finger at the bird. 'Oh . . . something tells me that you're all wet.' Huffily, Archimedes looked down at his damp ruffled feathers, then sulkily went back inside his house, slamming the door. An hour passed. Rain continued to slash the windows and drip from the roof but suddenly there came another, sharper sound. The loud blast of a horn rent the air and a horse whinnied. Merlin stroked his beard. Surely someone must be approaching the castle . . . and in such foul weather, too. He peered through a hole in the wall of the tower. Far below a rider on horseback was waiting to cross the drawbridge. Impatiently he sounded his horn again.

A sentry on the castle parapet called, 'Who goes there?'

'Pelinore! It's Pelinore, dash it all. Open up! I've got big news from London. Come on, man . . . drop the bridge!'

Minutes later the drawbridge was creakily lowered and the vibration made Merlin's rickety tower room shake. The magician was excited. 'Big news, eh?' He pulled his watch from the folds of his voluminous gown. 'Mmmm . . . I can't wait for *The Times*. The first edition won't be out for at least twelve hundred years.' Thoughtfully, he walked over to a pile of books. 'Archimedes,' he called softly, 'ah . . . would you mind sailing down there and . . .'

'Not interested,' came the huffy reply from inside the owl's private domain.

Merlin opened the small front door of the bird house and jiggled the tip of his magic cane inside. 'Oh, come, come, come now, dear Archimedes. You're as wet as you can get . . .'

'No!' The owl was obstinate in his refusal. Why

should he fly out into the rain?

Merlin peered in at the ruffled bird. 'I'll turn you into a human,' he threatened.

'Ha, you wouldn't dare!'

'Just try me. I will . . . so help me, I will!'

Sulkily, the owl emerged. The threat had worked. Oh, all right, I'll find out what I can,' he said ungraciously and, with a flash of wings, flew out of a window-slit into the damp night. Darkness had fallen early and the landscape looked gloomy and full of shadows. A few lights blinked from the lower castle windows and Archimedes managed to fly inside without being observed. Going directly to the stuffed deer's head where he had perched before, he settled on top of the antlers and waited.

Back in the tower, Merlin chuckled, hugging himself with glee. 'Ha, ha. It works every time. Just like magic. The threat of being turned into a human being is always too much for dear old Archimedes.' He too, settled down to wait.

From his perch, Archimedes surveyed the hall. Sir Ector was seated at the table drinking wine. Kay was seated across from him and Wart was busily engaged in clearing away piles of used dishes. Presently the front door was flung wide and Pelinore stood framed in the doorway.

Rising, Ector flung out his arms in a gesture of welcome. 'Pelinore! Greetings . . . greetings, old boy.' The knight removed his wet cloak, took off his gloves and approached his host. 'Now, what's all this noise about London, huh?' Sir Ector asked, filled with curiosity.

The two men shook hands and Pelinore then walked towards the grate where a few logs hissed damply, blowing out clouds of smoke but little heat. 'It's big news, Ector. Really big news.'

Sir Ector beckoned his unexpected guest to join him at the table in food and a jug of wine. 'Sit down, man, and let's hear all about it.'

'They're having a big tournament New Year's Day!'

Wart's ears instantly pricked up as he continued collecting dishes. 'Oh, that's not news, dash it all,' complained Ector in disappointed tones. 'They always do.'

Pelinore took a deep draught of wine. 'But here's where all the excitement comes in. To the winner of this tournament goes the *crown*!'

Ector choked in surprise, blowing a fine spray of wine into Pelinore's face. 'You mean . . . you mean he'll be King of All England?' His voice trembled with excitement.

Pelinore stood up, raising his jug of wine. He repeated solemnly, 'King of All England!'

Ector banged his fist on the table and roared at his son, 'Kay lad, did you hear that?'

Kay rocked back and forth on his chair. 'Ha, ha. Pretty fair prize, I'd say.'

Ector, kindled with enthusiasm, leapt to his feet. 'Yes, and *you* could win it boy, if you knuckled down to your training. We'll have you knighted by Christmas and then . . . off to London.' He slapped his son heartily on the back. 'What do you say?'

'Sure! Why not? Why not?'

Ector pointed to Wart standing at the table, a pile of dishes balanced in his arms, his eyes wide at the exciting news. 'Wart, lad, how'd you like to go to London? If you stick to your duties you can be Kay's squire.'

The boy's blue eyes flashed with happy surprise. 'Oh, sir, I'd love to go to London. I will work hard, I promise . . . I promise.' He hurried from the hall, his heart thumping with pleasure. Seconds later, a resounding crash echoed from the cellar's depths. Wart had tripped over with the dishes. Sir Ector and Pelinore looked at each other, and then both guffawed with laugher.

But Kay was angry, his face sullen. 'I don't want Wart for my squire.'

Ector and Pellinore were not listening. They were

too busy toasting each other. This was a night for celebration. 'Here's to London and here's to Kay and here's to the banner of the castle of the forest Sauvage, ah . . .'

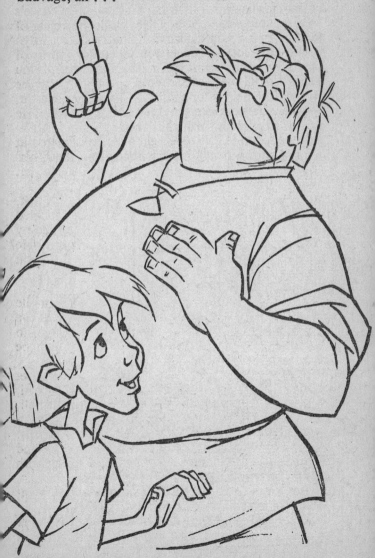

As the two knights became more and more tipsy, Archimedes gave a small hoot of disgust. He'd heard enough. Unnoticed he made his exit flying back to Merlin in the tower. The wizard eagerly awaited his news.

By the following morning the weather had cleared and Sir Ector was determined that his son, Kay, should have lots of practice in the art of jousting. Shortly after the sun had risen, Kay, dressed in heavy armour, was seated on a splendid horse. In his hand he held a long lance. 'Charge!' yelled Sir Ector. 'Put your weight forward. Lean into it. Steady . . . steady with the lance . . . oh . . .' He groaned aloud as Kay flew right over the castle wall, landing with a heavy crash of metal on the other side.

Merlin sat up in bed. 'What . . . what is going on, Archimedes? Archimedes . . . where . . . where are we?'

The door of the owl's house banged open and Archimedes, looking ruffled and sleepy, poked out his head. 'In a tumbled-down old tower, in the most miserable castle in all Christendom, that's where!' Snorting indignation, he crawled out on to his perch and shook out his feathers.

Merlin scratched his beard. 'Don't you even remember the boy?' asked the owl, crossly.

Merlin yawned. 'Ah, yes . . . the boy, the boy!'

From the grounds below, the sound of Sir Ector's booming voice floated upward. 'Can't you remember one blasted thing? A tight grip on the lance, Kay! It won't bite you.'

Merlin stretched his arms above his head and, climbing from the uncomfortable bed, walked sleepily to the tower window and peered out. Archimedes lifted up his perch, flew across to the window with it held in his claws and set it down beside the wizard. Kay had managed to climb back over the wall and, with a foul look on his face, was attempting to remount his horse. 'Loose in the saddle, knees in tight, weight forward, and stay on target,' instructed Ector.

Kay landed on the horse's back like a ton of bricks and the animal looked over its shoulder at the clumsy Kay, whinnying its annoyance. The boy jumped around like a young elephant. Sir Ector clucked. 'You keep losing your grip,' he snorted.

Pelinore came forward with advice. 'It's not just a matter of muscle, son. Jousting is a . . . a fine skill.' Kay appeared to be listening as he pulled his helmet down over his head. 'It's a highly developed science,' continued the knight.

From the tower window, Merlin said with loathing, 'Science indeed. One dummy trying to knock off another dummy with a bit of stick. A lot of rubbishy fiddle-faddle!'

'And Wart's just as hot for it as the rest of them,' Archimedes reminded the magician in cold tones.

In the field beyond the courtyard, Wart leapt lightly over a wheelbarrow, picking up a lance and, placing it in the jousting machine, fixed the machine's shield and helmet.

Merlin looked with pride upon the boy he intended taking under his wing. 'He certainly is. That boy has got real spark. Lots of spirit! He throws himself heart and soul into everything he does and that's really worth something . . . providing it can be turned in the right direction.'

'Ha, ha. Fat chance of that.' The owl was not optimistic.

Merlin leaned further out of the window. 'Oh, I plan to cheat of course.' The owl looked shocked. 'I'll use magic, every last trick in the trade if I have to,' continued Merlin. 'Yes . . . every trick in the book!'

CHAPTER FIVE

Later that same day, Merlin and Wart were walking along beside the moat. As usual, Archimedes was settled on the wizard's hat stretching his wings every once in a while and flying a few yards before returning to his favourite perch. Wart's serious little face was reflected in the water as he talked. 'I'd give anything to go riding about on a great white charger, slaying dragons and griffins and man-eating giants.' His voice was wistful.

Merlin smiled kindly at him. 'Well, and won't you?'

Wart shook his head. 'No. You see, I'm an orphan, and a knight must be of proper birth. I only hope I'm worthy to be Kay's squire. That . . . that's a big job, too, you know.'

'Well, indeed, yes. Yes! I would say almost impossible.'

Wart nodded, looking sad. He sat down by the moat, gazing into its depths. Merlin dropped down beside him as a fish jumped high in the air, its body a rippling gleam of silver. 'Humph . . . well now, lad, when I say that I can swim like a fish, I really mean *as* a fish.'

Wart's eyes grew large. 'You mean you can turn yourself into a fish?'

Merlin nodded. 'After all, I happen to be a wizard.'

'Could you turn me into a fish?' enquired Wart, from a kneeling position beside the water.

Merlin asked seriously, 'Do you have any imagination? Can you imagine yourself as a fish?'

Wart grinned. 'Oh, that's easy. I've done that lots of times.'

'Good: Then I think that my magic can do the rest.' Raising his cane, Merlin touched the boy lightly on the head with it. He frowned as though he had forgotten something. 'Archimedes, now what is that fish formula?' he asked.

The owl, who had been dozing, yawned and opened his eyes. 'Huh? What?'

'You know, that Latin business!'

The owl looked down at his master. 'If you don't mind I'll say good day to the both of you, if you please.' Flying off into a tree, he sat on a branch staring at them.

Merlin chuckled, whispering in Wart's ear, 'When he stays out all night, he's often grumpy next morning.'

Wart laughed, too. 'Ha, ha. Then he must stay out every night.'

Merlin joined in the merriment and Archimedes frowned disapproval on them both, convinced that they were laughing at him. The magician raised his arms. 'All right, boy. All set? Here we go!' He recited a mumble-jumble of strange words and again tapped Wart with his cane. A magic puff of dust caused Wart to vanish. The dust thinned to reveal a lively fish bouncing on the grass.

Kneeling, Merlin endeavoured to catch it but the fish leapt up, getting tangled in his beard. 'Am I a fish? Am I a fish?' Wart's voice came from the slippery creature.

'Yes, yes, yes, yes. You *are* a fish but if you don't stop that flippity floppin' around and ah . . . get into the water you won't last long.' Merlin crawled on his knees in a further effort to catch Wart as he leapt on to a log. At last, Merlin held the fish lightly in his hands and then dropped it into the moat. 'Now stay right there,' he said, 'and I'll be with you in a minute.'

Wart tried to propel himself in his new environment, but landed in some mud on the bottom. Merlin, now also disguised as a fish, swam to Wart's rescue, pulling him from the mudbank. 'So you thought you could take off like a shot, did you?'

'Well, I am a fish, aren't I?'

'You merely look like a fish,' replied Merlin. 'That doesn't mean you can swim like one. You don't have the instinct, so you have to use your brain for a change. You are living between two planes.'

A frog, sunning itself on a lily pad, stuck out its foot and tapped Wart as he swam past. Wart looked up as a beetle skimmed the water's surface. Seen from a fish-eye point of view, the moat was a very different place.

Merlin swam level with his small companion. 'Now, somewhere between the ceiling and the floor . . . there's a lot of ups and downs, like . . . like a helicopter.'

'A helicopter?' enquired Wart. 'What's that?'

'It's . . . oh, well no, never mind.' Merlin circled Wart moving his tail back and forth. 'Every flick of a fin creates movement. So . . . first we'll start with the caudal fin.'

Wart used his side fins and turned over. 'No, boy . . . your tail . . . your tail!' urged Merlin.

Wart swished his tail fin but bumped into Merlin. The wizard flashed ahead, Wart and the frog from the lily pad following. Merlin turned his head, explaining, 'That gives the forward thrust. Now come on, let's get a rhythm. Left and right, like day and night. That's what makes the world go round.' The two fish accompanied by the frog swam into a hollow log and Merlin sang:

In and out,
Thin and stout,
That's what makes
The world go round;
For every up
There is a down,
For every square
There is a round.
Ah, for every high
There is a low.
And for every to
There is a fro.
That's what makes
The world go round!

A fly landed on the surface of the water. Without pausing for reflection, Wart surfaced and swallowed it. Suddenly it dawned on him what he had done. 'Merlin, Merlin,' he cried in alarm. 'I swallowed a bug!'

'What's wrong with that? After all, my boy, you are a fish. Instinct, you know.'

'But you said I had no instinct.'

'Oh, I did?' Merlin smiled a fishy smile and broke out into another ditty:

> That's neither here nor there,
> The main thing is you must set
> Your sights upon the heights.
> Don't be a mediocrity;
> Don't just wait
> And trust to Fate,
> And say that's how
> It's meant to be;
> It's up to you
> How far you go,
> If you don't try
> You'll never know,
> And so my lad,
> As I've explained,
> Nothing venture . . . nothing gained!

Merlin and Wart both chuckled. 'Let's swim through that tall grass again,' suggested Merlin. 'It tickles, doesn't it.'

Still laughing, they swam towards it and swiftly disappeared amongst the floating reeds. Merlin backed into a catfish and hastily apologised. Wart giggled as the frog caught up with him. It was a curious frog who loved company. When Wart spied an old beer stein he swam inside but the lid closed and he was trapped. After a minute's wriggling he escaped through a hole in the bottom only to come face to face with a bullfrog. Startled, Wart leapt

upwards. 'Oh, you big bug-eyed bully, you,' he stormed angrily.

'Here, here, boy,' reprimanded Merlin. 'No sense going round insulting bullfrogs. A fish has plenty of problems without that. The water world has its forests and jungles, too.'

In the green, shimmering shadows a pike suddenly appeared, a large fierce-looking fish with a wide gaping mouth. So far, the wizard and Wart were unaware of the menace close by and the wizard continued talking as he swam beside his little friend. 'So it has its tigers and wolves. That's what makes the world go round.' He broke into song:

> You see my boy,
> It's nature way,
> Upon the weak
> The strong ones prey;
> The human life,
> It's all so true,
> The strong will try
> To conquer you.
> And that is what
> You must expect,
> Unless you use
> Your intellect,
> Brains and brawn,
> Weak and strong,
> That's what makes . . .

Merlin broke off at Wart's loud gasp. 'Oh . . . oh!' he choked. The wizard glanced hastily over his shoulder and a shocked expression registered in his eyes. The pike was at very close quarters. 'Help, Merlin, help!' shrieked Wart as the pike swished closer, his jaws open ready to clamp down on Wart, who was swimming away as fast as he could. His speed was no match for the bigger fish and Merlin snatched at the pike's tail in an effort to slow his progress. The pike snapped, narrowly missing the scared Wart. He shook free of Merlin and was off again in pursuit of a tasty meal. Merlin, anxious to help Wart, accidentally swam inside a helmet lying on the bottom of the moat. With a clang, the visor shut tight, trapping him inside.

Wart's predicament grew more serious with every passing second. How was he going to escape the hungry, determined pike? 'Quick, Merlin . . . oh, quick!' he shouted. 'The magic . . . use the magic!' Wart emerged from the shelter of a rock and darted to the helmet where Merlin was swimming round and round. From its cramped interior the magician called, 'Oh, no, you're on your own, lad. Now's the chance to prove my point. He's the brawn - you're the brain.'

Terror-stricken at these words, Wart fled right into the open. If he didn't take more care he would be eaten up after all. 'Don't panic . . . use your head and outsmart the big brute,' commanded Merlin from his tiny prison.

Wart struggled to calm himself and not to let fear keep the upper hand. Under the circumstances it wasn't easy! He led the pike towards a chain dangling in the water. The links were wide and Wart swam through easily but the pike caught his nose in the links.

From the visor, Merlin called out congratulations. 'Smart move, lad! That's usin' the old intellect!'

But Wart's problems were by no means over. After a vigorous struggle the pike managed to extricate his sore nose from the chain and, in bad humour, streaked off again to track down his intended victim. Wart, concealed behind a clump of reeds, peeked out nervously, hoping for inspiration. It came in the form of an arrow embedded in the silt at the bottom of the moat. Risking safety, he darted down, picked up the arrow in his mouth and hid again. Bubbles rose from the underwater growth as he swam around. The pike had seen the bubbles. Suddenly, fearfully, Wart found himself nose to nose with the hungry pike. In sheer panic he dropped the arrow, but made a quick flip to retrieve it. The large fish opened its jaws . . . and quick as a flash, Wart thrust the arrow deep inside.

From the helmet, Merlin called, 'Bravo, boy! Great strategy.'

Wart breathed a sigh of relief saying aloud, 'Oh dear, is this lesson about over?' He felt at the end of his tether as he swam towards Merlin's temporary refuge and peered in.

'Eh . . . did you get the point?' the wizard enquired.

'Yes . . . yes! Brain over brawn.'

Merlin nodded. 'Okay, lad. I'll fix the big brute.'

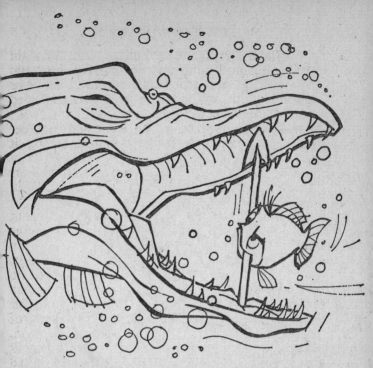

No sooner were the words spoken than the enraged pike appeared. He had managed to break the embedded arrow and free himself but pain and humiliation had merely added to his fury. More determined than ever to have Wart as a tasty snack, the big fish redoubled his efforts.

Wart surfaced in terror and leapt clean out of the water on to the grassy bank. To his dread, the pike followed. Wart gulped air, sure that his end had come. On a nearby tree, Archimedes was dozing. Perhaps it was intuition or Wart's plea for help which roused him, for he suddenly opened his eyes, blinked rapidly and spotted the two fish on the bank. 'Who is . . . why . . . it's that boy, still disguised as a fish, and he's got company! He's in real trouble!

'Help . . . help . . . oh help me!' gasped Wart in anguish.

Too late! The pike opened its jaws and Wart slid inside. But no . . . all was not over! Archimedes flew swiftly into action and retrieved the tiny squirming fish as the pike's jaws were about to close. Instead, they closed on the owl's toe. Wart thankfully flopped down the bank and into the water, swimming away from the shore as swiftly as

he could. The pike returned to the river still holding Archimedes. The owl flapped his wings as hard as he could and the pike finally released him. Huffily, the exasperated bird spurted a long fine spray of water from his beak and wiggled his sore toe. This was no situation for a dignified owl, he told himself as he drifted downstream. Wart, drawing level, leapt right over Archimedes before falling with a loud plop back into the water. The desperate pike, determined not to be foiled again, leapt in pursuit of Wart, knocking Archimedes beneath the surface with his powerful, swishing tail.

It was a game of catch as catch can. The pike chased Wart, the owl chased the pike, at the same time attempting to rescue Wart by picking him up in his beak. The owl again managed to catch the small slippery fish just before the pike's snapping jaws closed on him. Away flew Archimedes, Wart dangling from his mouth. Their last view of the giant pike was as it swam into a pile of rocks severely bumping its nose. Accidents were by no means over . . . Archimedes flew directly into a tree trunk, striking his head a blow which would give him a headache for some time to come. Wart dropped to the ground like a stone.

At that precise moment, Merlin surfaced, this time as himself . . . not a fish. Swiftly picking up his magic cane, he waved it over the pathetic fish flopping and panting on the grass. Wart was a boy again. Merlin peered into the depths, remarking, 'What . . . yes, what in thunder is a monster like that doing in the moat. I'll turn him into a minnow.' But of the pike, there wasn't a sign . . . not even a bubble. 'How in the world did you ever get out of that mess?' the wizard asked Wart.

Wart's breath still came in short, hard gasps. 'That . . . that awful big fish almost swallowed me and he . . . Archimedes, *saved* me!' Wart sounded not only grateful but surprised. He and the owl had not always been the best of friends

Poor Archimedes still lay on his head at the base of the tree into which he had flown, a fountain of water issuing from his beak. Merlin picked him up and stroked him gently. It didn't take the bird long to revive. Managing to crawl weakly on to a limb, he shook out his damp feathers and snorted, 'Save him? I did nothing of the sort. I intended to eat him. Young perch is my favourite dish. You know that!' He glared at Merlin and the boy.

Merlin laughed. He knew Archimedes - gruff and grumpy outside, but warm and soft as marshmallow inside. 'Do you believe him, Wart?' he asked.

Wart looked puzzled. Had Archimedes really meant to eat him? The boy didn't understand the owl's moods as well as Merlin did.

'Wart? Wart?' The boy looked round. In the distance he could see Sir Ector calling him. He would have to go.

Turning swiftly to the magician, he said, 'Thank you, Merlin. It was so much fun . . . an' Archimedes, I . . . I want to . . .'

'Oh, pinfeathers, boy!' said the owl, cutting short what he knew would be thanks. He fanned out his wings to dry.

'Wart . . . Wart, where are you?' Ector's voice was becoming impatient.

'Coming. I'm coming!' yelled the lad with a final wave to Merlin and his wise bird, he dashed off in the direction of the castle.

As the little figure vanished into the distance, Merlin turned to Archimedes with a half smile. 'Now . . . why would you half drown yourself for a titbit of fish, eh? And after such a big breakfast.'

Self-consciously, the owl rolled himself into a ball trying to wring himself out, then fluffed his wings again. The magician stroked the bird's head, Archimedes hopped on to the wizard's hat and the two of them turned in the direction of the castle.

CHAPTER SIX

Later that same afternoon, Wart was talking excitedly to Sir Ector while Kay loafed in the background, listening with an expression of disbelief. 'Oh, we were doing fine until we got into deep waters. Then along comes this huge pike with big jaws and sharp jagged teeth . . .'

'Oh, turn him off, dad,' said Kay irritably.

Wart, ignoring Kay's unkind remark, gestured with his arms. 'He was a monster. The biggest fish I ever saw.'

Ector looked down his nose at the small lad. 'And boy, that's the biggest fish story I've ever heard.'

Wart looked crestfallen. 'But it's true, sir!'

Ector leant forward shaking a finger in the boy's face. 'That's three demerits for being late - and three more for the fish story.' He pointed to the dark cellars. 'Now hop it to the kitchen.'

Wart lowered his head sadly. Sir Ector never wanted to listen and on rare occasions when he did, Wart was made to appear a liar. Glad in one way to escape, the disheartened boy ran towards the kitchens.

When he had gone, Kay placed his hands on his hips and laughed mockingly. 'I told you Wart was looney.'

Ector shrugged. 'He's either out of his head or there's something mighty fishy going on around here.'

Down in the gloomy kitchens, Wart had lots of chores awaiting his attention. Unwashed dishes were stacked high on the table, whilst piles of dirty pots littered the giant-sized fireplace, its grate large enough to roast a whole ox. The sight was a depressing one. As he started scrubbing a greasy pan he sang to cheer himself up:

> For every high there is a low,
> For every to there is a fro,
> To and fro . . . stop and go,
> That's what makes the world go round.

A noise alerted the boy and he looked up expectantly. Merlin was tapping his cane on an iron kettle. Wart's long face changed into a happy smile of welcome. 'Oh, it's you, Merlin, sir!'

Merlin watched the boy working. 'Have you ever considered being a squirrel,' he asked.

'Well, no!' exclaimed Wart, surprised by the question and turning his attention to another dirty kettle.

'Ah, well, now there. It's a tiny creature with enormous problems. How he has survived throughout the ages is one of nature's biggest mysteries. His life is hazardous, downright dangerous, in fact.' Merlin paused. 'Would you like to try it?'

Wart didn't answer. Surrounded by a multitude of unwashed dishes and pans, his chores were at present much more of a reality than thoughts of being a squirrel. 'Ah, it's too dangerous for you, eh?' commented Merlin tapping again on a kettle.

Wart paused, glancing up. 'Oh, no, it's not that. It's just that I've got six demerits and all this work to do.' He looked hopelessly at the chaos surrounding him.

Merlin stroked his beard. 'What a mess,' he agreed. 'What a medieval muddle. We'll have to modernise it. Start an assembly line system.' Wart was scarcely listening . . . he didn't have the time.

Merlin stood up on a stool, rapped his cane against its side to command attention and waved his arms in the air. 'All right now,' he said, gazing round the untidy kitchen, 'now all pay attention!' he mumbled an incantation. The effect was startling. A brush in the washing tub swirled the water into foamy suds; plates stacked themselves and under Merlin's direction marched in an orderly line into the soapy water where the brush scrubbed them clean. A bucket filled itself with fresh water to rinse the dishes and a pair of bellows, working unaided at top speed, dried them off.

Wart ducked out of the way, his blue eyes looking large as saucers as dishes moved over and round him. This was the type of magic he really appreciated. 'But I'm supposed to do it,' he whispered in awe.

Merlin had other ideas. 'No one will know the difference, son. Who cares as long as the work gets done.' He laughed and clapped his hands as the washed dishes stacked themselves. The magician was fully aware that there were more interesting things in life than the drudgery of kitchen chores for Wart. Determined that all would be left in excellent order, he set two brooms to sweeping the littered floor and two mops to dunking themselves in suds to mop the greasy flag-stones. Merlin nodded and looked round the kitchen. Sir Ector would not be able to find any fault with the clean, orderly kitchen when he inspected it. The room sparkled. 'Come on, son, let's go,' he said, with a happy chuckle. 'Let's go!' Wart needed no extra urging. Grinning, he ran out of the kitchen followed by the wizard. As they walked out into the fresh air, Wart counted himself fortunate in having such a wonderful friend.

Man and boy trudged towards the woods and the warm sun tinted the trees with a green and saffron light. A jay screeched wildly as they stepped on to a mossy path. Smiling, Merlin produced his cane, ready to perform further magic. Within an instant, both he and Wart were transformed into bright-

eyed, bushy-tailed squirrels. Wart peeked round at his magnificent brush of a tail with mounting excitement. Life with Merlin was never dull!

Unable to control his enthusiasm, the changed boy raced up a tree and leapt on to a branch. What fun it was . . . he leapt again. 'No, boy, no!' Merlin's warning came too late. The branch was dead and Wart fell into space. Just in time he caught hold of another. 'Now, what did I tell you,' scolded Merlin. 'Always look before you leap.'

Wart shook himself. 'Well, I made it, didn't I!'

The magician joined Wart on the tree limb. 'Yes, yes, you made it . . . you made it. But you can't always trust to luck, lad. Now watch.' The wizard braced himself for a leap. 'Now, first you start on the short jumps. Gauge the distance carefully and . . .' To demonstrate he took off into space, but almost missed the branch. Wart darted forward to help. 'Oh . . . oh dear . . .' breathed Merlin breathlessly. 'Now, you see? Even after careful calculation, you can still miss.' He shook himself. 'Don't take gravity too lightly or it will catch up with you. Gravity is what causes you to fall.'

'Like a stumble or a trip?' asked Wart.

'No,' corrected Merlin. 'It's the force that pulls you downward. The phenomenon that any two particles . . . or bodies, if free to move . . . would be accelerated towards each other.'

The explanation was too complicated for Wart to follow, so he moved along to another bough. His action brought him face to face with a cute girl squirrel. Deliberately, she blocked his way chattering loudly and bouncing up and down in glee. Wart was nonplussed at this unlooked-for situation. He tried to squeeze past but the girl squirrel had no intention of letting him escape. Wart looked anxiously over his shoulder. Where was Merlin? The wizard appeared from a thick cluster of leaves. 'Oh, Merlin, how will we get by?' pleaded Wart, with a worried expression on his face.

Merlin peered over Wart's bushy tail at the third party. 'Well, I . . . I suppose we'd better go back to a side track.'

'Go on . . . go on, you've got lots of room,' Wart told the newcomer. But she was determined not to move and wanted to be friendly . . . too friendly for Wart's comfort. Coming closer, she nuzzled up against him. Wart tried to break off, nearly falling.

Merlin couldn't repress a smile as he scratched his head with his front paw. 'Heh! Well, I . . . I guess she can't be side-tracked. That's a girl squirrel, lad, and a *redhead* at that!' He gazed at the furry bright-eyed creature in admiration. She was not only determined, she was pretty, too.

Wart was at a loss. In an effort to make her move, he pushed his nose against hers. Accepting this as an invitation she placed both her front paws on his face. Wart knocked them down . . . she put them back. This went on for several minutes with Merlin an amused spectator. Chattering loudly, the girl squirrel finally broke away, beckoning Wart to follow. She ran up and down the branch, stole a swift glance over her shoulder, returned to Wart and when he didn't follow . . . ran off again. In puzzlement he watched her antics. 'She sure acts funny,' he remarked to Merlin.

'Oh, she likes you!'

The red-headed squirrel tried to lure Wart again, for she was a young lady with a strong will and had no intention of being side-tracked. Wart slid behind Merlin in an attempt to hide but she slithered after him, nearly causing them all to fall from the security of their branch. 'Well, well,' began Merlin, 'that's nature again. But I'm afraid there's no time to explain.'

Wart turned tail in a desperate attempt to flee. Lunging forward the girl squirrel dragged him back. He struggled. Merlin shrugged philosophically. 'You're on your own, lad. I'm afraid magic can't solve this problem.'

By now, the girl squirrel had wrapped Wart in her bushy tail and was kissing him. Trying desperately to draw away, he blurted out, 'Look, I'm not a boy squirrel. What I mean is I'm not a squirrel at all. I'm a *boy*!'

The girl squirrel, chattering happily, ignored his remarks and kissed him again. Angrily, Wart threw her tail into her face and moved backwards. Girl squirrel peeked provocatively from beneath its bushy splendour. It was too much for Wart. In fright he sought Merlin's protection, pleading, 'Merlin, what'll I do? She won't leave me alone!'

Girl squirrel watched and giggled. 'I'm afraid you're stuck, lad,' replied the magician, unhelpfully. 'When a squirrel chooses a mate, it's for life.'

Wart rubbed a paw across his furry face. 'But I won't be a squirrel tomorrow.'

Merlin shrugged, acknowledging the fact. 'But she doesn't know that . . . she only knows one thing for sure. That you're a him and she's a her.'

With a triumphant laugh, the girl squirrel rushed forward flinging her arms round Wart. Once more he tried to fight her off but her resolve was strong. As he made a futile attempt to hide, she dragged him along the branch by his tail. Poor Wart! He felt trapped. Merlin twitched his furry whiskers and began to sing:

It's a natural phenomenon,
It's a state of being, a frame of mind,
It's a most befuddling thing;
And to every being of every kind
It is discombooberating.
You're wasting time resisting,
You'll find the more you do,
The more she'll keep insisting
Her him has got to be you.
It's a rough game, anyone knows;
There are no rules, anything goes!
There's no logical explanation for this . . .

The sun moved slowly through the trees and the girl squirrel kept up her incessant pursuit, not to mention her chattering. Wart felt desperate. If Merlin wouldn't help him, he'd have to try to help himself. Recklessly he raced along branches, then took a flying leap landing on a branch dangerously low to the ground. It was particularly menacing, for at the base of the tree lounged a wolf with his mouth hanging open. Alerted by the noisy rustlings above he looked up expectantly. The red-headed squirrel gasped in horror, thrusting her paws across her eyes. She couldn't bear to look. Wart had slipped and was rapidly slithering down the tree trunk towards the ground. But an obstruction was at hand to save the luckless Wart. An owl, looking after her nest of young, was sitting placidly in the fork of a thick branch when Wart landed on her hand with a crash. Startled, she blinked and looked up.

'Who . . . who did it?' she squawked angrily.

Wart backed away from her fury, accidentally tripping over the nest. A large, fluffy baby bird pecked him hard. The owl was outraged at being disturbed by a clumsy squirrel. 'Now go on . . . shooo . . . get a tree of your own,' she ordered. To press home the point she pecked Wart on the head twice. The owl meant business and Wart had no desire to prolong his acquaintance for a moment longer than necessary. The angry bird spat out a mouthful of fur plucked from Wart's head, glaring at him in a most unfriendly fashion. Wart backed away feeling highly unpopular, but his red-headed lady friend soon let him know he was still more than popular with her. He was her Mr Right! Popping up beside him again she grabbed his tail with a firm paw. He wouldn't escape this time if she could help it! The owl gave the pair of them a dirty look. 'Whoooo . . . I . . . oh, you squirrels!' she finished up in exasperation.

Dangling carelessly from a higher branch, Merlin watched the scene, an amused glint in his eye. 'She's gaining on you,' he called mockingly to Wart as the game of chase recommenced. Merlin picked an acorn considering whether or not he should eat it. Deciding against the temptation he sang in timbre tones:

> There's no sensible explanation
> For this discombooberation,
> It's a most hodge-pogical
> Most confusiling, most bamboozling,
> Most befuddling, ah, ah, thing . . .

Dragonflies hovered and birds chanted in unison but the catchy tune had attracted another listener, with unexpected results for the magician! A granny squirrel popped her head out of a tiny hole in the tree-trunk, looking at him with bright, admiring eyes. She advanced hesitantly at first, and then, in a sudden rush, darted forward, embracing the startled Merlin and wrapping him lovingly in her tail. He choked and spluttered in alarm. 'What the . . . ah, here now, miss. I mean madam . . .'

'Ahhhh . . .' murmured granny squirrel as she stroked his cheek.

Merlin, trying his best to keep calm and look dignified, handed her back her tail with a gracious

gesture. 'Now, you ah . . . you've made a mistake!
Now, now please . . .'

If he wasn't prepared to co-operate, granny
squirrel was more than willing to make the moves.
Chattering in his ear she possessively picked up his
bushy tail. Merlin did his best to explain. 'Ah, look
here. I am not a boy. I mean . . . I mean I'm not a
squirrel at all.' Balancing tiny spectacles on the tip
of his nose he said in his best dignified manner, 'I
am an old man!' Granny squirrel merely squeezed
him. 'I mean I'm an old *human*. Understand?'

To granny squirrel this was a joke. She
considered it very funny and to prove it she kissed
Merlin's nose with a great display of affection. It
was too much. Wiping his damp furry face the

6

magician spluttered, 'Ah . . . oooooh . . . oh, hang it all. Now please . . . please go away. Shooo . . . shooo . . .' He grunted loudly to show displeasure but, to his acute annoyance, this seemed only to encourage her. Playfully, she knocked him down on the branch so that his spectacles fell off, then she hid her face in her tail, laughing helplessly. Merlin seized this opportunity to creep stealthily away. He didn't get very far. Showing great agility for an older squirrel she raced after him tickling his back with her tail. Merlin felt despair . . . now he knew how Wart had felt. Briefly, he wondered where the boy was.

Wart appeared as if by magic, looking breathless and worn out. As the magician and the boy faced each other, Wart blurted, 'Merlin . . . *please!* I'm tired of being a squirrel. It's nothing but trouble.'

Merlin scratched his ear. 'Oh, you think you've got troubles? Look at my . . . ah, look back there.' Granny squirrel was using Merlin's tail like a powder puff, brushing it lovingly over her face. Snatching it ungraciously from her paws, Merlin tucked it under his arm, pushed past Wart, knocking him from the limb, and took off like a rocket.

Wart was forced into another dilemma. Managing to seize a branch as he fell, he soon found that his choice had been an unlucky one. An ominous crack announced that the wood was rotten and unlikely to support him. The hungry wolf still loitered beneath the tree hoping for a reckless move on the part of one of the squirrels. When the bough did break, striking his head, he was momentarily dazed. Unfortunately for Wart, his bushy tail caught beneath the bough, which was now a splintered mass lying on the ground . . . and the wolf had his foot on it. How to escape? The wolf shook himself, noticed the squirrel and licked his chops in anticipation. A meal at last! But the red-headed squirrel had no intention of seeing her Mr

Right serve as a snack. She proved herself more than just a playmate. Like lightning, she jumped from the tree, brave and uncaring of her personal safety. Fiercely she bit deep into the wolf's hind leg. He yelped in pain. Turning, he snapped at her with savage jaws but she was smart and took off in the direction of the cliff nearby. He followed . . . and it was his undoing. She leapt into the air towards another tree, he also leapt . . . right over the cliff edge. Rolling over amidst a pile of freshly cut logs at the bottom he whimpered as she glared and shook her tiny paw in a gesture of defiance and fury. How dare he attack her boyfriend?

The rolling logs finally pitched the wolf into a pond at the bottom of the slope. The girl squirrel gave a cluck of satisfaction at this and went back to seek her mate. She found Wart very shaken by his near brush with death, sitting a trifle breathlessly in the fork of a tree. It seemed safer than many of the branches. Chattering words of comfort, she hugged him lovingly, fussing over him and stroking his face. Wart would have been very ungracious had he not hugged her in return.

Merlin was fed up. For him the chase was still on, as granny squirrel, amorous and determined as her grand-daughter, was still stroking his cheek. 'I've had enough of this nonsense,' he exploded. Dropping down into thick foliage he disappeared in a puff of smoke. In place of a squirrel stood a man in a purple cloak and a tall violet-coloured hat rising to a point.

Granny squirrel blinked in disbelief and then screamed, over and over again. Her scream told of vexation, fear and frustration. She could scarcely credit the evidence of her eyes. 'There, now you see, I'm an ugly, horrible, grouchy old man,' the magician said to the disappointed creature. Frightened, granny squirrel ran away and sought refuge in her little home near the top of the tree trunk. The day had proved both odd and very disappointing. Her tiny house was cosy and certainly roomy enough for two. Sadly, she shut her front door, her hopes dashed.

Wart, still in an ardent embrace, looked down and saw Merlin on the ground. 'Quick . . . quick, Merlin,' he shouted. 'The magic!'

He escaped and raced down the tree and in a sudden puff of smoke a small boy appeared with a girl squirrel perched on his knee. 'There, now you see,' explained Wart to the sweet red-haired squirrel with treacle-brown eyes, 'I'm not a squirrel . . . I'm a *boy*!' The squirrel began to sniff in distress. 'I tried to tell you that I was a boy - a human boy.'

Tears showered down the squirrel's furry face, falling like dewdrops on to her chest; her small shoulders heaved in misery. She didn't want a human boy - she wanted her boy squirrel back, her playmate! Wart felt upset. 'Oh, if you could only understand,' he said softly. Turning her back, she climbed nimbly up the tree and from a tiny hole in the trunk looked down on him. She was still crying.

Slowly, Merlin and Wart sought out the woodland path and made their way towards the sunlit fields and the distant castle. Even from a distance, Wart could still hear the girl squirrel's persistent sobs. He bit his lips in perplexity, for he was a kindly boy and hated to cause hurt.

Merlin nodded his head in understanding, his voice sympathetic when he spoke. 'You know, lad,. that love business is a powerful thing.'

'Greater than gravity?' asked Wart, his eyes serious.

'Well, yes, boy . . . in its way. Actually, I'd say . . . yes, I would definitely say that it's the greatest force on earth.'

Wart had learned a strange lesson!

CHAPTER SEVEN

Sir Ector and Kay were out on the field adjoining
the castle. Ector was trying rather ineffectually to
put his son through his paces. If the boy was to
stand an even chance of winning the tournament in
London to qualify for the title of king, he had a lot
of work to do. Both men were holding swords, Sir
Ector shouting instructions in a booming voice,
hoping that it would penetrate his son's dull senses.

Suddenly, the air was rent with the screams of a
kitchen maid. Her lank hair streaming untidily
behind her, she rushed towards the field shouting,
'Sir Ector . . . oh, Sir Ector. The kitchen.'

Ector raised his eyebrows, clearly annoyed at
being interrupted by a kitchen wench. 'Hold it,
son . . . hold it. Kay, I say . . .'

'Black magic all over the place,' yelled the
woman, panting as she drew level with the men. Her
eyes were wide with terror.

Kay, about to make a lunge, refused to be foiled
by the maid's arrival and swung his sword.
Harassed and vexed, Ector clubbed him over the
head, knocking him to the ground. He tutted his
annoyance. That boy was the giddy limit! Turning
with a frown to the maid, Sir Ector asked gruffly,
'Now . . . now, what's all the commotion, huh?'

Breathlessly, the woman pointed. 'Oh, sir . . .
the kitchen. It's under an evil spell.'

'Ah! I bet it's that old goat, Marvin.' Ector
turned to Kay, who had struggled to a sitting
position on the ground and was pulling off his

helmet. 'Come on, son . . . I knew he'd give us trouble.' Ector followed the woman in the direction of the kitchens, Kay bringing up the rear. When the knight descended the stone steps he stopped short in amazement. Something very strange indeed was going on. Fantastic masses of bubbles floated through the door and danced into the air, glinting with rainbow hues in the late afternoon sun. Thrusting them aside, Ector entered the kitchen. The spectacle which met his eyes caused him to clap his hands to his head. 'Black magic . . . definitely black magic of the worst kind,' he yelled, as he viewed dishes marching through a tub, brooms

sweeping the floor and pans stacking themselves. When Merlin had departed for the woods he hadn't switched off his magic spell. Sir Ector raised his sword in anger and as Kay chose that precise moment to push his way through the door, he caught another blow on the head. This time he was not wearing his helmet. 'Ouch . . . ouch,' he cried, rubbing the huge bump which had instantly formed.

Sir Ector was in a fury. He had ordered young Wart to do the chores and now he knew that the magician had been at work to help the boy. How dare he? Ector's orders . . . his authority was being challenged. In a frenzy of rage he charged into the kitchen. Right and left he struck with his sword, battling with pots and frying pans. His sword broke and to his indignation he was pushed by the pressure of marching dishes right into the wash tub where he was vigorously scrubbed by a busy brush.

'Heaven preserve us,' shrieked the kitchen maid, clapping her hands to her cheeks in horror.

Kay used his sword to duel with a broom but he came off worst and was punched on the nose. Other brooms jumped into the attack and then a mop entered the fray. Wrapping itself round the young man's neck it pulled him down and commenced mopping the floor with him while the brooms beat him on the back. Heaven knows what the final outcome might have been had not Merlin arrived at that moment.

Glancing inside the kitchen doorway he asked, 'Now, what have we here?'

Wart, close on his friend's heels, looked horrified. This meant trouble with a capital T. 'Jumpin' hoptoads,' he breathed, standing closer to Merlin.

The magician raised his arms, although there was more than the suspicion of a twinkle in his eye. 'Ala Ka . . . ' he chanted and within a few seconds he had completed his incantation.

A flash of lightning filled the room, dishes

clattered to the floor and all activity ceased. Wart drew a long breath and waited for the wrath that was sure to follow. He didn't have long to wait.

Sir Ector struggled to climb out of the giant-sized tub and Kay, who had flung aside the soaking mop, went to his father's assistance. Being clumsy as usual he fell into the tub himself. His eyes blazed with fury . . . it was the last straw!

Sir Ector, water running down his face, turned to Merlin with a black scowl that would have terrified a lesser man. 'Oh, so there you are, you old goat. Well . . . what's the idea of flinging your evil spells all over the place?' He spat out a mouthful of suds and bubbles. 'Well?' he snapped. 'What have you got to say for yourself, huh?'

Calmly, Merlin faced the enraged knight. 'You call washing dishes and sweeping floors a work of evil?'

The magician's calm, unruffled air only served to incense Sir Ector. 'I'll decide what's right and wrong around here,' he yelled. 'Besides, that's the Wart's job. It's one of his duties.' Picking up the broken half of his sword he pointed it savagely in Wart's direction. 'Look here, boy. If you want to make that trip to London . . . you'd better toe the mark.' He thrust the fragment of blade close to the frightened boy's face.

Before Wart could reply, the kitchen woman, courageous now that Sir Ector was on the spot, ventured close to Merlin and shook her fist at him. 'You old goat. If I ever catch you in my kitchen again, I'll . . .'

Merlin froze her with one look. 'Oh, no, madam, you won't,' he said coldly. Her courage ebbed and she stepped back. In the next instant, Merlin had vanished without trace . . . without even a puff of smoke to indicate where he had gone.

For a long moment, no one spoke. Ector was the first to recover from his surprise. 'Well, by jove . . . ' he began.

'We oughta run that old geezer right out of the castle,' said Kay grimly, glaring at Wart who was still standing close to the doorway and looking lost.

'No!' Ector was decisive. 'He might cast an evil spell on the lot of us. Turn us into stone. Shhhh . . . no telling what the old devil might do!'

Wart advanced into the kitchen, ready to jump to his absent friend's defence. 'He's not an old devil. He . . . he . . . he's good. And his magic is good, too. If you'd leave him alone.'

Ector glowered down at the small boy, wondering at his audacity. 'Now, look here, Wart. That's three demerits.'

'Box his ears, dad!' cut in Kay, spitefully.

Despite the hostile atmosphere, Wart spoke up valiantly. 'Just because you can't understand something it doesn't mean it's wrong.'

'Ten more demerits!' roared Sir Ector.

Tears flooded Wart's eyes and spilled down his cheeks. 'You make all the rules an' nobody can say anything!'

Ector stamped his foot on the damp floor. 'You've said a-plenty, boy!' He coughed, exuding a few more bubbles. 'All that poppin' off just cooked your goose. Kay, from now on . . . young Hobs is your squire.' He strode across the floor. 'Did you hear that, Wart? Hobs is going to be Kay's squire.'

Wart's face fell. All his dreams, his hopes had been dashed. 'Yes . . . yes, sir.' He traced the pattern of a flagstone with his toe to hide the stream of tears welling afresh.

Kay smirked and said, 'That'll teach you to pop off, ya little pipsqueak.' As he passed a broom handle he slashed it in half with his sword. The door slammed after him and Wart was left to his own devices - a sad, lonely boy.

Darkness had long since fallen but Wart felt so despondent that he had not even bothered to light one of the torches that usually flared from a wall socket. The fire was almost out and mechanically he shoved a small log into the grate, then dropped his head back on his hands. Outside, a chill wind, blowing in fitful gusts howled mournfully and cold night air blew along a draughty passage. Wart had not eaten, but he had no appetite for food; bitter disappointment ate deep into his heart. He had banked so much on going to London, on being Kay's squire. Now there seemed to be nothing to look forward to.

A light flared, throwing long, mysterious shadows into the corners of the kitchen and suddenly, there was Merlin seated on an upturned bucket! His kindly face was set in lines of sympathetic understanding. 'I'm sorry, lad. Sorry that I spoiled everything. I know that trip to London meant a great deal to you.'

Wart, though glad of Merlin's company, still felt thoroughly miserable. With bowed head he whispered, 'Oh, it . . . it's not your fault. I shouldn't have popped off. Now I'm really done for.'

Merlin gestured expressively with his hand. 'Oh, no, you're in a great spot, boy. You can't go down now . . . you've hit rock bottom. It can only be up from here.'

'I'd like to know how!' Wart was unconvinced.

Merlin tapped the boy lightly on the head with his cane. 'Use your head. An education, lad that's what you require.'

'And what good will that do?' asked the boy.

Merlin shrugged. 'Get it first, then who knows? Ah . . . eh, are you willing to try?'

Wart lifted up his head and heaved a deep, troubled sigh. 'Well, at this point, what have I got to lose?'

Merlin stood up and patted him on the back.. 'That's the spirit. We'll start tomorrow. We'll show 'em won't we?'

Still looking doubtful, Wart nevertheless answered, 'We sure will.'

On the following morning, Wart climbed the rickety stairs up to Merlin's tower to start his education. The magician was waiting and in preparation had a map spread over the table, a pile of books stacked in readiness and his round globe standing in the centre of the room. Archimedes was sitting on top of it, looking very wise.

Merlin greeted his little friend with enthusiasm. 'First of all, lad, we've got to get all these medieval ideas out of your head.' He pointed to the globe. 'We must clear the way for new ideas.' Wart sat down beside the round ball with strange designs covering its surface and peered at it. 'Yes,' continued Merlin, 'knowledge of man's fabulous discoveries in the centuries ahead. Now that would be a great advantage, boy.'

'Advantage indeed!' hooted Archimedes in disapproval. 'If the boy goes about saying the world is round, they'll take him for a lunatic.'

Wart blinked in disbelief. 'The world is round?'

'Yes . . . yes, that's right.' Merlin spun the globe to demonstrate with the owl travelling slowly on top. 'And it also *goes* round.'

Wart pointed excitedly. 'You mean it'll be round some day?'

'No,' answered Merlin patiently, '. . . it's round now! Man will discover this in centuries to come, and he will also find that the world is merely a tiny speck in the universe.'

'Universe?' Wart scratched his head. The word was new to him.

Archimedes flapped his wings expressing impatience with Merlin and his methods. 'Ah . . . you're only confusing the boy. Before you're through he'll be so mixed up he'll . . . he'll be wearing his shoes on his head. Man has always learned from the past. After all, you can't learn history in reverse.'

Merlin puffed on his pipe and blew out a cloud of smoke, his face growing angry. Archimedes could

be very difficult at times. The owl continued, 'It's confusing enough, for heaven's sakes.'

Merlin wafted a giant cloud of smoke in the owl's direction. It billowed around him so that he became a dim, shadowy creature, hidden in the bluish haze. The bird spluttered and coughed, flapping his wings in annoyance.

'All right. Have it your way, Archimedes,' replied Merlin at length. The magician crossed the room and sat on a chair close to the door. 'Very well. You're in charge. You're the headmaster now. From this moment, Wart is *your* pupil!'

Archimedes and Wart exchanged long, questioning glances.

CHAPTER EIGHT

In the past, Archimedes had often given the impression that he disapproved of Merlin's interest in Wart, yet he soon demonstrated that he was an excellent teacher. Once having made up his mind to coach the lad, he set to with a will. Fixing Wart with his unblinking tawny eyes he said, 'From now on, boy . . . you do as I say.'

Wart nodded obediently. 'Yes, sir.'

'All right!' Archimedes perched atop the globe of the world and indicated a massive pile of books. 'Now to start off, I want you to read these books. That, my boy, is a mountain of knowledge.'

Wart took a dismayed step backward. 'But . . . but I can't read.'

Archimedes stared, dismay written on his face. 'What? What?' he repeated. 'And I don't suppose you know how to write?'

Looking and feeling a little guilty, Wart shook his head. The owl hooted. 'What do you know! Well . . . well . . .' He made a decision. 'Never mind . . . never mind. We'll just have to start at the bottom. The ABC.'

A little later, the owl was perched on Wart's head as the boy stood at the blackboard trying to form letters of the alphabet. After a few tries, he managed 'A' and 'B'. The owl nodded approval. 'Now make a loop and go round to form a "C",' he coached.

Wart looked pleased at his effort. Glancing over his shoulder he called out to Merlin who was rummaging through a drawer searching for one of his models. 'Merlin . . . look, I can write.'

The magician smiled as he looked at the board. 'Yes, that's pretty good!'

Archimedes was not so impressed. 'Henscratch, that's all. Henscratch. Now, come on.'

When Wart came to the letter 'G' he wrote it backwards. Archimedes, still sitting on the boy's head, showed his disapproval by stamping forcibly on his pupil. 'No . . . no . . . no! Now use your head . . . use your head, will you? How do you ever

expect to learn anything? You've got to concentrate!'

Merlin couldn't find the model he was searching for. Stroking his beard, he turned to the owl. 'Archimedes, have you seen that . . . ah . . . that flying model?' Spreading his arms, he flapped them to demonstrate an aeroplane.

The owl drew himself upright with a disdainful sniff. 'I have nothing to do with your futuristic fiddle-faddle, you know that.'

Turning his attention away from the blackboard, Wart looked round, pointing towards the ceiling. 'What's that thing hanging up there?'

'Oh yes . . . of course. Here we are!' Merlin beamed as he spied the model above his head. He took it down.

Wart was fascinated as he watched Merlin spin the propellors. 'You mean men will fly one of those someday?' he asked in wonderment.

'If man had been meant to fly, he would have been born with wings,' remarked Archimedes, flapping his own to prove the point.

Merlin wound up the plane's propellor. 'I am about to prove otherwise, Archimedes, if you care to watch.' Merlin raced across the room, the plane in his hand. Unfortunately, his long silver beard caught in the propellor, winding it round and round. 'Oh . . . oh, dear . . .' he cried, running so hard that only in the nick of time did he save himself from falling out of the window. His beard dangled down the outside wall as he attempted to unravel the aeroplane from it. The little model, its propellor still whirring, dived downwards, falling into the moat below with a noisy splash.

It was too much for Archimedes. He laughed so much he had to hold his sides. 'Man'll fly alright,' he muttered between fresh bursts of mirth. 'Yes, like a rock.'

Merlin stroked his tangled beard. 'It would have worked if . . . if it weren't for this infernal beard.'

7

Assuming a calm air of dignity, he walked from the room, his footsteps echoing on the rickety staircase. When he returned, the owl was still laughing. He hadn't enjoyed himself so much in a long time.

Unperturbed, Merlin lit his pipe, always a comfort at a trying time. 'Man will fly someday, I tell you. I've been there. I have *seen* it.' The magician's tone was emphatic, allowing no room for doubts.

Wart had been leaning out of the window watching roosting birds in a pink cloud of blossom on a thicket. Two scolding blackbirds on the grass were quarrelling over a worm, and in the azure sky a group of brown sand martins swooped and dived eagerly for insects. At Merlin's words, Wart turned back into the room. 'Oh, I do hope so! I've always dreamed about flying.' He stared out of the window again, his face wistful, his voice dreamy. 'I've dreamt many times that I was a bird and that I could go sailing all over the sky, completely free and high above everything.'

While he was speaking, Merlin put down his pipe, tiptoed over to his cane and, coming up behind Wart, touched him gently on the head. Instantly, the boy was changed into a bird.

Wart was delighted. Jumping up and down on the windowsill he said joyously, 'It's my favourite dream. Oh . . . but I suppose everybody dreams about flying. I'm a bird . . . I'm a bird . . . gosh . . . I'm a bird!'

Merlin laughed at the boy's evident delight. Wart was already trying his wings, taking off in little flights from the window. Hastily, Merlin grabbed him. 'Hold it boy. Not so fast . . . not so fast!' He took a deep breath. 'First, I'd better explain the mechanics of a bird's wing.' Wart watched as Merlin used Archimedes' wing to demonstrate. 'These large feathers are called the primaries . . .'

The owl snorted huffily. 'And since when do you know all about bird's wings?'

'I have made an extensive study of birds in flight . . . and I . . .' Merlin's explanations were cut short.

Archimedes puffed out his chest. 'And if you don't mind, I happen to be a bird.'

Merlin prodded Archimedes with his finger. 'All right, mister know-it-all. He's your pupil!' Putting Wart down on the window-ledge the magician walked away.

So to Archimedes fell the task of tutoring Wart in the art of flying, as well as teaching him to read and write. Looking solemn, the owl said to the boy, 'Now, boy, flying is not merely some crude mechanical process. It is a delicate art, purely aesthetic. Poetry of motion.' To demonstrate, he twirled round on one foot, wings outspread. He peeked over the ledge. 'And the best way to learn is to do it. Now since we're pretty far up, we'll start with a glide. Spread your wings . . .'

Wart spread his wings and fanned out his tail, anxious to begin his first lesson. 'Now,' said the owl, and together the two birds took off from the ledge, first gliding down, then levelling out.

'Now, tuck your feet under like me,' instructed Archimedes.

Urgent rushing air glittered in the sun's rays as Wart rose high, lifted by a playful breeze. As suddenly, it dropped him and he found himself falling . . . falling . . . 'Don't fight the air currents,' warned the owl who was keeping a close watch on his charge. Nodding, Wart flew on. He breathed deeply. This was really living. Never before had he experienced such a feeling of freedom . . . of buoyancy . . . From his vantage point he could see the hills sloping steeply downward and the tops of the trees in the wood. They resembled a giant patchwork quilt worked in varying shades of green and copper. A hare crouched on the horizon and then vanished with one mighty leap into a clump of bushes. The waters of

the moat sparkled, birds flew in and out of a clump of reeds. Wart began to somersault, swoop, dart and glide. The owl looked worried but soon his expression changed to one of pride. 'Why, boy, you're a natural,' he called. 'Ho, ho, ho.'

With a pleased 'Cheep . . . cheep,' Wart hovered above a fragrant bed, bright with blossom. Bees swarmed and droned around him as they searched for honey.

'Are you sure this is the first time you've ever . . .' The owl broke off, his eyes widening in sudden fear. Long wings cast a menacing shadow. 'Hawk . . . hawk . . .' screeched Archimedes. The cry was taken up by the other birds, their long terrified shrieks flung upwards, vibrating in the air.

All the birds scattered at the warning. Fear spread like a fungus. Smouldering with suppressed violence and carrying the fear of instant death, the dreaded hawk zoomed low. 'Look out, boy! Heads up!' warned the owl. The hawk dived towards Wart.

'Help . . . Archimedes . . . help,' screamed Wart, terror stricken.

Swiftly, the owl grabbed the hawk's tail feathers and hung on, so that the great bird's talons narrowly missed Wart. The boy flew faster but the hawk was in hot pursuit. Archimedes was left with a tail feather in his mouth. Wart flew towards the wood, hoping to find cover or a place of safety. All the other birds had taken refuge. As the hawk disappeared into the wood's dark foliage, small creatures remained in hiding. When they finally emerged there was a new alertness and a wariness amongst them.

But Wart was not out of danger. Frantically he looked for a hiding place for the hawk was flying just above the trees, ready to pounce again.

At that exact moment, Wart spotted a cottage tucked away in the centre of the wood, possibly a haven of refuge. Diving towards the thatched roof he landed on the chimney hole, panting loudly. The hawk's slender body and pointed wings slashed the air. Wart had no time to think . . . to choose another place. He dived straight inside the chimney stack . . . into a cloud of stifling smoke. 'Oooolffff! Ohhhhh . . . whoa . . . ' he cheeped. Smothered in soot he landed in the fireplace . . . a bedraggled and scorched bundle of feathers. Fate had decreed that Wart should be saved from the hawk, but now he had landed on the hearth of Madam Mim, a powerful and very dangerous witch!

CHAPTER NINE

Mad Madam Mim, seated at a table in her dingy cottage, was playing solitaire. From the pile of ashes on the hearth, Wart coughed loudly in an attempt to clear the soot from his throat. The witch threw down her cards, grinning unpleasantly. 'Sounds like someone's sick. How lovely! I do hope it's serious. Something dreadful.' She got up, peering round the room and presently her eyes

alighted on Wart, sitting in the fireplace. 'Oh, bat gizzards,' she exclaimed in disgust. 'It's nothing but a scrawny little sparrow with a beak full of soot.' Picking him up she held him at arm's length and looked at him for a moment before dropping him, completely disinterested.

Wart, who thought her a very odd looking creature, with her shock of unruly red hair, funny upturned nose, skinny arms and long black dress, said as loudly as he could, 'Oh . . . oh . . . I'm not really a sparrow. I'm a *boy*!' Shaking himself, he flew on to the table and dusted off his feathers. 'Merlin's changed me with his magic,' he boasted. 'He's the world's most powerful wizard.'

'Merlin!' Madam Mim's voice held contempt. 'The world's most powerful bungler, you mean. Why, boy, I've got more magic in one little finger . . .' She ceased talking for a moment and pranced about the room. 'Ha, ho, now don't tell me you've never heard of the marvellous Madam Mim?'

'Well, no,' Wart was forced to admit. 'I guess I haven't!'

Archimedes peered in through the dusty window. Catching sight of Wart, his tawny eyes widened in alarm. 'Madam Mim! Oh, good heavens . . . good heavens . . . this is a catastrophe!' Hastily he backed out of sight. The witch's evil reputation was known all over the countryside, and she was a person to be feared. Of all places for Wart to have chosen as a refuge! The owl sighed. How was it, he wondered, that that boy managed to get into so many scrapes? Archimedes decided he had better tell Merlin of this dangerous situation immediately.

Madam Mim felt that she had been challenged and was determined to prove that she had a stronger brand of magic than Merlin. With Wart as her captive audience she whirled round the room with the speed of a spinning top. 'I'm truly marvellous,' she boasted to Wart as she sang in a cracked voice:

With only a touch I have the power,
To wither a flower, ho, ho . . .
I find delight in the gruesome and grim . . .

'Oh, that's terrible,' interrupted Wart in shocked tones.

Madam Mim accepted his remark as a compliment to her skills.

'Thank you, my boy, but that's nothing for me.' She sang another line of song:

'Cause I'm the magnificent
Marvellous Mad Madam Mim!

Dropping Wart a curtsey, she said unexpectedly, 'Do you know what? I can even change size.' As proof of this she began to grow taller and taller until her head was in the rafters, banging on the ceiling. 'You see, I can be huge. I can fill the whole house.' Her leering smile was unpleasant and Wart shivered in fear. He was impressed by all this yet he was a little afraid of the ugly old woman and wished that Merlin was with him. Hopping across the table he stood beside a coffee cup. Mim sensed his discomfort and laughed, a high-pitched screech that sent chills down his back. To his amazement, the unpredictable hag suddenly shrunk in size until she was even smaller than Wart. Crouching on the table amongst the playing cards, she grinned, then disappeared from view. Moments later, she reappeared with a broom in her hand. In a cracked voice she sang:

I can be teeny,
Small as a mouse,
Black sorcery is my dish of tea,
It comes easy to me
'Cause I'm the magnificent
Marvellous Mad Madam Mim.

Dramatically, Mim threw her broom to the floor, slid on to it and flew round and round the room. Diving low over the table, she buzzed Wart, brushing his tail feathers as she swished past. He hopped on to the top of a candlestick. Laughing wildly at her captive's discomfort she buzzed him again, flying round his head in circles. He felt dizzy. Unexpectedly, she dived off the table, resuming her normal size.

Wiggling a long crooked finger, she smirked, 'Did you know that I can make myself uglier yet?'

Wart, still balanced on the candlestick said rudely, 'Oh, that would be some trick!'

Shoulders heaving with silent laughter, Mim pulled her unruly hair right over her face then swept it back. Her features were indeed uglier than ever . . . completely hideous. Wart jumped in terror as the witch shook with malevolent mirth. 'You see, I win! I win! Aren't I hideous, boy? Perfectly revolting?'

Wart could only nod his head in dumb agreement. There was no arguing on that point. 'But you ain't seen nothing yet,' continued Mad Mim in a bragging tone. 'Just watch!'

Fascinated in spite of his fear, Wart stared in astonishment as the witch changed into a beautiful young girl, more enchanting than any he had ever seen. It was confusing. Mim sang again, only this time her voice was as fair as her face:

I can be beautiful,
Lovely and fair,
Silvery voice,
Long purple hair,
But it's only skin deep,
I'm an ugly old creep . . .

Coyly, she stroked Wart under the chin. Embarrassed, he pulled back. In a flash, Mim was her ugly old self again. The witch moved over to the table, poking Wart in his feathery chest. 'What do you think, boy? Who's the greatest?'

Wart had been put on the spot. 'Well, ah . . . Merlin's magic is always . . . well, useful . . .' he said nervously. Mim gave a nasty smile. 'Er, I mean he uses it for something good,' faltered Wart.

Mad Mim tugged her hair. 'And he must see something good in you! Yes . . . and in my book that's bad!'

Crossing to the dusty windows where cobwebs lingered, she slammed the shutters. The room, already grim and gloomy, was now dark as a pit. Mim's voice echoed from the deep purple shadow. 'So . . . my boy, I'm afraid I'll have to destroy you.'

There was no denying that her electrifying words came as a terrible shock to Wart. Already frightened and wishing he had found anywhere but the witch's cottage in which to hide, he now fluttered in terror. How could he hope to escape? Panic-stricken, he flew on to the back of a chair. The mad witch advanced towards him and even in the darkness, he could see her evil eyes glowing. 'Yeah . . . I'll give you a sportin' chance. I'm mad about games, you know.' Her cackle changed to a long, low hiss. Mim was now a cat . . . a huge black menacing cat ready to pounce on its victim. Shivering like a leaf in the wind, Wart tried to fly . . . and found he couldn't move. The cat leapt, landed on the table missing Wart, and slithered to the floor overturning a chair. In a desperate bid for freedom, Wart flew on to a china cabinet, but the cat sprang up, overbalancing an earthenware vessel. In the shadowed room it fell to the ground with a resounding crash, breaking into fragments. Mad Mim laughed, a blood-curdling sound, and Wart's tiny frame trembled. Would he ever get out of this alive? He had serious doubts. Flying blind, he came to rest on the bull's-eye of a target board. His heart was beating so loudly he was sure the mad witch could hear it. Whether she could or not scarcely mattered for her great cat's eyes could see very well in the dark. With a savage 'miaow' she knocked Wart to the ground with a fierce satiny paw. 'I win,' she spat, picking Wart up unkindly in her talons. She squeezed him and in the next moment had turned herself again into the witch. The cat had vanished.

Shaking Wart she held him at arm's length, her face hard and cruel. His small body shook in alarm. He sent out a silent plea for a miracle. 'I win,' mouthed the old hag again. 'The game's over. Why, you little devil, you. I'll wring your scrawny little neck.'

Wart closed his eyes in an agony of fear. So he was to die after all. Without ever growing up . . . without seeing the jousting in London or ever being a squire. It was to end in this miserable cottage in the heart of the wood. He took a deep breath - and waited.

But instead of Mad Mim's fingers closing round his throat, the cottage door was flung wide admitting welcome sunlight and fresh air . . . but of far greater importance, it also admitted Merlin. The magician stood framed in the entrance, his wise old eyes sizing up the situation. Mim was sitting on the floor with Wart in her hands, a pile of broken earthenware at her feet. 'What . . . what the devil are you up to?' asked Merlin angrily.

Crafty Mim changed her attitude, stroking Wart's head with a none-too-gentle hand. 'Merlin! Of all people! Ah, well, you're just in time. He, he, he . . . we were playing a little game.'

'She was gonna destroy me,' shouted Wart indignantly.

Mad Mim jumped to her feet, still clutching the bird. Placing him on the table she turned on Merlin and slapped his face - hard. Eyes flashing with thwarted fury, she screeched, 'And just what are you gonna do about it? Wanta fight? Wanta have a wizard's duel?'

Thus challenged, Merlin said with infuriating calm, 'As you wish, madam!'

'Well, come on. Step outside!' With an aggressive gesture, Mim pushed past Merlin and waited in the forest clearing. At last . . . at long last, there was to be a showdown between the evil witch and the wonderful wizard. Merlin followed Mad Mim from the cottage and she picked her way deep into the woods. Wart followed, fluttering nervously in the background, alive with curiosity and yet fearful, too. He didn't understand what was going to happen. Yet one thing he knew for sure. Merlin's timely arrival had undoubtedly saved his life. Wart perched on the branch of a tree and to his surprise and delight, Archimedes joined him a moment later.

The owl looked enquiringly at the witch and wizard, then asked, 'What . . . what's up boy? What's going on?'

Wart turned to the owl. 'They're going to have a wizard's duel. What's that mean?'

Archimedes hooted in concern. 'Oh dear, it's a battle of wits. The players change themselves into different things and attempt to destroy one another.'

'Destroy?' Wart's voice filled with alarm. Merlin was his friend - he didn't want him to come to harm, and all because Wart had fallen down the witch's chimney. It made him feel responsible.

The owl flapped his wings. 'Ah, just watch, boy . . . just watch. You'll get the idea.'

Mim led the way, trekking determinedly along the woodland path. Her presence had a startling effect on the wild life. A badger, blundering noisily through the undergrowth, went suddenly silent; a blackbird, singing in the high green light of a tree, stopped its burst of sweet song and uttered a shrill, warning note; a rabbit, hopping happily in a clump

of ferns, hastily dived for cover. The animals and birds of the woodland had an instinctive feeling of distrust when Mad Mim was about. The witch stopped, turned to Merlin and with one of her long crooked fingers flipped his beard aside. 'Now first of all, if you don't mind, I'll make the rules.' Her voice indicated that she fully intended making them whether Merlin agreed or not.

Archimedes whispered to Wart, 'Rules indeed! Ha . . . why she only wants rules so she can break 'em.'

Mim's ears were sharp. Angrily she scowled towards the tree where the two birds were watching. 'I'll take care of you later . . . featherbrain!' she croaked. Archimedes practically choked with wrath. How dare she describe him . . . the educated owl . . . as a featherbrain! It was a deliberate insult.

'Ah . . . rule one,' continued Mim, staring hard at her opponent. 'No mineral or vegetable . . . only animal. Rule two, no make-believe things like ah . . . oh . . . pink dragons and stuff.' Stepping closer, she spitefully tweaked Merlin's nose. 'Rule three, no disappearing.'

'And rule four is no cheating,' interrupted Merlin annoyed at having his nose pulled.

The two powerful magicians, each with wizadry at their fingertips, stood momentarily back to back. Then, as Merlin marched in one direction, the unscrupulous Mim disappeared.

Wart was furious that the old crone was cheating from the start. 'Merlin! She's disappeared,' he cheeped warningly.

Merlin looked over his shoulder, his face growing dark with anger. Out of the air a vicious-looking crocodile formed, chomping ominously with its strong, broad jaws. Quick as a flash, Merlin disappeared inside his hat, his voice echoing from space. He uttered a hasty incantation, then called, 'Now, Mim, *you made the rules*!'

Disguised as a crocodile, the witch cackled evilly. Reaching inside Merlin's hat she brought out a turtle . . . Merlin's first disguise. She flung the turtle to the ground and it landed on its back with a dull thud. The turtle grunted in alarm as Mim crawled towards him. Pulling on a strong blade of grass, Merlin managed to right himself. Being a turtle on your back was not comfortable at any time . . . and under present circumstances, highly dangerous!

'Change to something else, Merlin,' yelled Wart from his perch.

'Ah . . . ah . . . yes, yes! Just give me time to think, boy.'

Mad Mim crept even closer. Merlin started to chant a strange-sounding string of words, but then realised he'd forgotten the spell.

8

'Quick, Merlin, hurry!' warned Wart.

'Come on . . . something bigger,' encouraged Archimedes from the safety of the tree.

'Oh, no . . . something smaller,' advised Wart.

'No disappearing,' screeched Mim, disregarding her own breach of the rules. Already, she decided on a transformation. She took on the form of a rhinoceros, whilst Merlin turned into a crab. It wasn't the wisest choice. 'Just you wait,' she laughed. 'So you want to play rough!'

Before Merlin had the opportunity to make another move, he was in trouble. 'Oh . . . oh ouch!' he groaned, as the rhinoceros butted the crab and lifted it high in the air on the tip of its horn. It was a bad moment for Merlin. With an air of triumph, Mim charged towards a broad tree trunk, Merlin spiked aloft. 'Right, Merlin, I'll smash you, you old crab,' she shrieked with delight. Merlin shuddered. The tree was only feet away from the cruel horn and thundering hooves. With difficulty, he managed to extricate himself from the horn, race down the galloping animal's back and jump clear, landing on a patch of moss. It softened his fall . . . and only in the nick of time. The woods rang as the rhinoceros galloped into the tree at full speed. Even the tree leaned over with the impact. Thwarted again, Mim screamed in sullen fury.

'Here I come, Mim,' taunted Merlin, altering his disguise to a billy-goat. Now it was his turn to charge the rhinoceros, who had her horn deeply embedded in the tree trunk and was a prisoner. Mim looked over her shoulder groaning, 'Merlin . . . Merlin . . . you wouldn't dare!'

'Just wait and see,' chuckled Merlin who knew that there was no point in being a gentleman when you were faced with someone like Mad Mim. She deserved all she got. Taking fierce pleasure in his mission, the billy-goat charged. Repeatedly, Merlin rammed and butted the rhinoceros who was struggling to free itself. An ominous crack rent the air and suddenly both the tree and the rhinoceros slipped over a cliff disappearing in a murky pool. Breathless, Merlin breathed a sigh of relief. The victory was surely his! But his rejoicing was short-lived.

A grotesque dragon emerged from the disturbed bubbling waters of the pool. Spitting fire and flame, it rose spreading scaly wings. It flew to the top of the cliff, belching smoke and leering horribly. Merlin, still in his disguise as a billy-goat, looked thunderstruck. This was against all the rules. 'Now, now, Mim,' he complained. 'No dragons . . . we agreed there were to be no dragons! Remember?'

Heat encircled the fiery beast. It snorted. 'Did I say no *purple* dragons; did I?'

Merlin blinked angrily at the wily witch. She had specified no pink dragons, then artfully assumed the form of a revolting purple dragon with bright yellow scales. That wasn't playing the game at all! Merlin rebuked himself for having trusted the words of the unscrupulous witch. He should have known better. Nevertheless, his immediate concern was to protect himself from the hot wrath of this fiery monster. Already, his billy-goat coat was singeing as the dragon emitted clouds of smoke and flame. He ran . . . but where could he hide? Frantically, his eyes searched the undergrowth. Perhaps he could turn into a mouse. There were numerous tiny bolt holes in the trees and rabbit burrows.

He made a decision and became a mouse and immediately tore down a hole. Snorting furiously, the dragon sent a blast of flame after him, singeing his tail. The hideous monster's fierce breath blew him right through the hole and out of the exit at the far end. Up . . . up into the air he went. To his horror, he smelled burning and discovered that his tail was on fire. Twisting like an acrobat even as he soared through space, he tried to blow out the flame . . . just as the dragon snatched him. His heart sank. Holding him firmly in her horny claw, Mim rejoiced, sniggering and guffawing in turn as she lauded her victory over the now helpless creature she was clutching. By grasping Merlin so hard she had extinguished the fire in his tail . . . but what use now? It looked as though Merlin was defeated . . . for good!

Stunned at the rapid turn of events, Wart and Archimedes sat petrified on the tree. It was hard to believe that the evil dragon had killed dear Merlin. Eyes brimming with tears, Wart opened his tiny beak. 'Oh . . . ohhh . . . that horrible old witch. I'll peck her eyes out.' He flapped his wings ready for flight, but the owl caught him, pulling him back,

'No . . . no, Wart, it wouldn't do any good,' he said sadly. 'It's too late.'

The loathsome dragon opened her claw, grinning with malevolence. She looked hard. Merlin wasn't there. She looked at the ground and over her shoulder, a very puzzled look. Where could he be?

The two birds were just as puzzled. 'He's gone!' said Wart, scarcely able to accept the evidence of his own eyes. 'Where *could* he have gone?'

The dragon looked nervous. She belched more smoke but her heart wasn't in it. She suspected a trick! Merlin *could* be devious, and in her heart she had to acknowledge that he was a master of the art of magic. From the dragon's still extended claw, Merlin's voice floated into the ether. 'Madam, I have not disappeared. I am *very* tiny. I am a germ. A rare disease . . . and *you* have caught me . . . yes, *caught me*, Madam Mim!'

Wart and the owl exchanged delighted glances. Merlin had played his ace card and shown his superiority. Wart wanted to sing out in triumph . . . but Merlin was still speaking. 'First, you break out in spots, followed by hot and cold

flushes. Then sessions of violent sneezing will attack you . . . and wear you down.'

Trapped and furious, Mim spat one giant sheet of flame after another, illuminating the shady woods. 'Watch it . . . watch it, boy,' warned the owl ducking to avoid a spurt of fiery sparks which had charred their tree.

Mim screamed in sheer frustration. She was beaten . . . there wasn't a thing she could do now to retaliate. Already she was feeling sick . . . and, horror of horrors, starting to break out in great ugly, red blotches.

Within the hour, Madam Mim, too sick to make further protests, had returned to her cottage. She had resumed her witch's form but the attack by the

strange germ had made her uglier than ever. Lying in bed, she cursed and moaned, mouthing secret spells. They were completely ineffectual against the rare virus.

Merlin stood over her, a thermometer in his hand. 'Oh ... it's not too serious, madam. Mmmm ... you should recover in a few weeks.' Wart and Archimedes hopped about on the bedspread, for they had been immunised from danger by Merlin. 'Yes,' continued Merlin with a faint smile, ' ... and in time you will be as good ... ah ... I mean as *bad* as ever. But in the meantime, I would suggest plenty of rest, and lots of sunshine.' Right on cue, a slanting sunbeam shone through the dusty window, illuminating Mim's spotty face and shock of hair. Covering her face with her locks she mumbled rebelliously, 'I hate sunshine . . . I hate horrible loathsome sunshine.'

Calmly pocketing his thermometer, Merlin ignored the witch's outburst. It was time to leave. The two birds flew on to the crown of his tall hat. At the door of the cottage he bowed slightly to Madam Mim and then stepped out into the clearing. As the threesome travelled the cool, mossy path, Mim's voice followed them. 'I hate it . . . sunshine, I hate it, I tell you . . . I hate it!'

Merlin shrugged and hurried on his way. Soon the distorted screams could no longer be heard. Wart cheeped in relief. 'You were really great, Merlin,' he said in admiration, 'but you could have been killed.'

Merlin nodded. 'True, lad but it was worth it, if you learned something from it.'

'Oh, I did . . . I did,' replied the tiny bird with enthusiasm. 'Knowledge and wisdom is the *real* power!'

'Right you are, Wart, so stick to your schooling, eh, boy!'

The drowsy afternoon subsided into a song-filled evening as the birds chorused in the air, fragrant with woodland scents. Long purple shadows announced the arrival of dusk. A robin trilled sweetly from a hedgerow as they reached the newly harvested fields. Suddenly the evening star appeared twinkling like a jewel in the heavens. Merlin nodded his satisfaction. It was an excellent omen!

CHAPTER TEN

The arm of winter held the countryside in a vice-like grip. Snow blanketed the fields and transformed the hedgerows into weird shapes. The moat was frozen over and the castle outlined against the sky. In the glow cast by spluttering, fiery torches held secure in iron wall sockets, Wart crossed the great hall and pressed his nose to the window. Snowflakes danced, flinging themselves recklessly earthwards. A chilly blast of air made him shiver and he hastily retreated. There were dishes to collect from the table where Sir Ector and Kay were dining with Pelinore.

It was a special occasion, as Kay had recently acquired the status of a knight. The timbers echoed with Sir Ector's great guffaws of laughter. In another room voices were lifted in song and there was a general air of merriment. Everyone was celebrating, except for poor Wart, who faced the cheerless prospect of another evening spent in the kitchen scouring dishes. Quietly, he tiptoed back to his duties, not wanting to rouse his guardian's displeasure.

Several months had passed since the duel between Merlin and Mad Madam Mim . . . months in which Wart had worked hard at his studies. The magician and Archimedes had been good tutors and Wart a more-than-willing pupil. Kitchen chores still formed a part of the boy's daily routine, but it was no more than he had grown to expect.

As Wart commenced stacking used dishes, Ector and Pelinore raised their glasses for a toast. 'Here's to victory in London for my son, Kay,' declared Ector proudly.

Kay, slouching untidily in a chair, said sternly, '*Sir* Kay, if you don't mind. I've been knighted, don't forget!'

Good humouredly, Sir Ector patted his son on the back. 'Of course, son . . . of course. It's your right!'

Ector poured more wine from a flagon. 'Here's to Sir Kay. Who knows? Possibly, the future king of all England.' He stood up, accidentally slurping wine over Kay's head, much to the new knight's annoyance.

Beneath his breath, Pelinore muttered, 'Kay the king? Ugh! What a dreadful thought!'

No sooner had Sir Ector sat down again when one of the kitchen women ran from the cellar, her face flushed with importance at being the bearer of bad news. 'Sir Ector,' she cried excitedly, '. . . Hobs has come down with the mumps. His face is all puffed up like a toad.'

Wart pricked his ears up at this unexpected turn of events. Hobs was promised as Kay's squire in the coming tournament. Ector shook his head. 'Gadzooks,' he roared. 'What a blasted inconvenience. Kay will need another squire, hang it all.' He stroked his chin and stared reflectively at the slim, blue-eyed lad collecting dishes. 'Wart, you're it!' he thundered.

'I'm . . . I'm what, sir?'

'Kay's squire. You're going to London, boy!'

Wart felt thrilled. It was the best, most exciting news he'd ever had. 'Yes sir,' he replied, his voice trembling with joy. Snatching up a pile of plates, he hurried towards the cellar steps, anxious to pass on his good news. A second later he tripped and fell. There was a loud crash as the dishes shattered and rolled down the stairs. He didn't even wait to pick them up, but rushed towards the rickety tower where Merlin still lived with Archimedes. A thought flashed through his mind and he retraced his steps, rummaged in a trunk and slipped a garment over his head. Then he raced again up the mean, twisting staircase. Bursting into Merlin's room, Wart extended his arms, shouting excitedly, 'Merlin, look . . . look I'm a squire!' His flushed cheeks and bright eyes showed his happiness.

Merlin, shivering as he sat huddled over a poorly lit stove, looked up with a frown. Archimedes hooted from his perch, ready with instant congratulations. 'Oh . . . ah . . . very nice, boy!'

Wart nodded eagerly, waiting for Merlin's comment. The magician took a long time answering and when he did, his tone conveyed sharp disapproval. 'Yes, indeed. A fine monkey suit for polishing boots . . .'

Wart's face fell. He stared down at his costume. 'It . . . it's what all the squires wear,' he answered defensively.

Merlin rose from his chair and faced the boy, his anger clearly marked. 'And I thought you were going to amount to something. I thought you had a few brains.' Thoroughly cross, he kicked the globe of the world with his foot, smashing it to smithereens. Wart looked bewildered. He hadn't expected this reaction from the wizard. He didn't understand. 'Yes,' continued Merlin in a severe voice. 'A great future as a stooge for that big lunk, Kay. Congratulations, boy!'

'What . . . what do you want me to be? I'm a nobody. You . . . you don't know a thing about what's goin' on today . . . ' The tremulous tones suddenly broke and Wart dissolved into tears. His face reddened. 'I'm *lucky* to be Kay's squire.'

Merlin brushed his hands through his silver beard, pulled his hat firmly about his ears and announced, 'Of all the idiotic things I've ever heard . . .' Spluttering in fury he muttered an incantation. A smoke cloud rose up around him. 'Blow me to Bermuda!' he ordered. Before the astonished eyes of Wart and Archimedes, the magician shot like a rocket through the hole in the ceiling out into the dark snowy night and freezing air.

Boy and bird rushed to the window and peered out, in time to catch a glimpse of Merlin flying across the sky.

Wart looked puzzled and crestfallen. 'Where did he go?'

The owl shook his head and returned to his perch. 'To Bermuda, I suppose.'

'Where's that?'

The owl flapped his wings, staring from bright tawny eyes at his friend and companion. 'Oh, an island way off somewhere. Actually, it hasn't been discovered yet!'

Wart didn't attempt to puzzle over that surprising announcement but enquired, 'Will he ever come back?'

Archimedes shrugged. 'Who knows? Who knows anything?'

Deflated by the magician's swift disappearance, Wart tramped dejectedly down the stairs, his good news suddenly gone sour. Life without Merlin would never be the same.

However, he did not have time to dwell upon the matter for a few days later, to his intense excitement, he found himself for the first time in the magic aura of London. Never before had he seen so many people gathered in one place, a noisy jostling crowd who squabbled, swore, drank and gazed about them in open-mouthed wonder. The tournament field was gaily decorated and bright with flags and bunting blowing in the breeze and despite crisp cold weather the sun shone thinly from a pale blue sky.

Wart was standing close to Sir Ector and Kay when a man with a deep booming voice stood on a raised platform, held his hand aloft for silence then shouted, 'For the crown of all England . . . let the

tournament begin.' A great cheer rose from the crowd as though from one mighty throat. As the din subsided, a flag was raised . . . the tournament had begun! Wart stood on tiptoe, trying to see over Kay's head. Two knights thundered on to the field; one in white armour and riding a handsome white charger, the other clad in sombre black and mounted on a great black stallion. Carrying long lances and protective shields, the men rode swiftly towards each other, urging their horses to battle. The crowds held their breath as back and forth the two knights charged, manoeuvred and jousted, each trying to knock the other from his horse. Tension mounted . . . both competitors were powerful men and betting lay heavily in favour of the one in white carrying off the title of victor. There was a moment's respite and the knights prepared to face each other on another charge. This time they crashed together while the horses whinnied and snorted their protests. The two knights fell to the ground.

'You see, Kay,' said Ector nudging his son. 'Now they are dismounted and will battle it out with their swords.'

Ector's words had the effect of making young Wart turn pale. Looking frightened, he tugged hard on Kay's sleeve. Irritably, Kay looked down at his squire. 'What is it?' he snapped.

Wart bit his lower lip in vexation. 'I . . . ah, ah . . . I forgot your sword.'

'Forgot my sword?' yelled Kay in exasperation, causing several people to turn and titter at the white-faced boy.

Wart stepped back a pace. 'I left it back at the inn!'

'Why, you . . .' The angry knight swung a stick at the boy's head but Wart leapt clear, jumping over a pile of equipment. Kay in his wrath didn't notice it and tripped, falling heavily. In fury he shouted from the ground, 'Bungling little idiot. You'd better get it or don't dare come back!'

Wart had never seen Kay so angry. Swift as a gazelle, he took off in the direction of the inn, Archimedes flying along at shoulder level. The boy breathed a sigh of relief as the lodgings where they had spent the previous night came into view. Wart pounded furiously on the black oak door. 'Let me in,' he cried in desperation. 'Please . . . let me in!'

The owl, sitting on the window sill, peered inside. All was silent and there wasn't a soul in sight. The tables were cleared, the tankards and flagons washed and hung in orderly rows from oak beams.

Archimedes shook his head. 'It's no use, boy. They've all gone to the tournament.'

'Oh dear, what'll I do?' Wart's anguished cry was full of despair. Without a sword, he daren't return to the field. 'Kay's *got* to have a sword,' he insisted, looking at Archimedes for suggestions.

The owl pointed with his wing tip. 'Well, look boy, look! There in the churchyard!'

Wart didn't hesitate but vaulted over a fence and sprinted towards a huge boulder on a grassy verge. In its centre a sword was plunged right to the hilt.

The owl shook his head. 'You're gonna have a time pulling it out. It's in so deep. Better leave it alone!'

'But Kay's got to have a sword,' insisted Wart. 'Somehow I've got to remove it.' A handful of people, who had not gone to the tournament but were loitering in the hope of easy pickings from strangers, stared in astonishment at the small fair-haired boy and the owl. Wart approached the sword and a strange blue light flashed from the handle, making him jump back in fear. Desperation urged him to try again. The blue light flashed a second time, more vividly than before. Driven by fear of Kay's fury, Wart gritted his teeth and seized the handle. To his astonishment, it slid from the stone as easily as butter. He was in too much of a hurry to notice the stares of astonishment, hear the gasps of wonder and fear which followed him as he dashed triumphant from the churchyard, holding the gleaming sword aloft.

9

Breathless, Wart arrived in the nick of time. Sir Ector turned proudly to his son. 'You're up next, lad. Better get ready.'

Wart thrust the sword into Kay's hand. The knight examined it then announced, 'This is not my sword!'

'Hold on, Kay . . . wait a minute.' Ector seized the sword and read aloud the inscription. 'Who so pulleth out this sword . . .' His voice was tinged with wonder. 'Oh . . . oh . . . it's the sword in the stone.'

The black baron who earlier in the day had fallen from his horse came forward and took the sword from Ector's hand. 'Here . . . let me see that!' He too read the inscription. 'The sword in the stone! Why, it can't be!'

'But look, it is!' shouted Sir Ector, in great excitement.

Pelinore's face was filled with wonder. 'It is . . . it's the marvellous sword.'

'Hold everything!' boomed the black baron. Turning towards the milling throng he yelled at the top of his lungs, 'Someone's pulled the sword from the stone.'

The words had an electrifying effect. Those who were closest listened in disbelief; grooms stopped brushing their horses. Had the miracle happened at last? Who had pulled the magic sword from the stone?

Ector bent towards Wart. 'Where did you get it?' he asked.

Wart blushed, unable to understand all the confusion. 'I . . . ah . . . ah . . . I pulled it out of the anvil that was on the stone.'

A score of knights burst out laughing. Wart's face turned a deeper shade of red. 'In . . . in the churchyard,' he explained.

'Very funny,' shouted someone with a sneer.

'The lad's a young Samson,' commented another.

Ector turned purple with rage, grabbing young Wart by the collar. 'You're making a fool of us, boy. Now tell the truth.'

'But I did, sir . . . honest I did,' stammered Wart unhappily.

'Then come on, prove it! Back to the stone with you.'

A group of knights and interested bystanders followed the irate Ector, the scoffing Kay and the terrified boy back to the churchyard. With as much dignity as he could muster, Sir Ector placed the sword carefully back in the stone, plunging it deep, right up to the hilt. 'All right, boy, let's have the miracle.' He nodded at Wart to repeat his previous performance. Wart crossed his fingers, then rolled up his sleeves and reached for the handle, but Kay's armoured hand suddenly stretched in front and seized Wart's wrist in a fierce grip.

'Wait a minute! Anyone can pull it out once it's been pulled.' Smugly, he pushed Wart aside. Ector pounded his fists with glee. It was the moment he had long dreamed of . . . glory for his son. 'Go to it, Kay,' he encouraged. 'Give it all you've got!'

Kay pulled . . . and pulled . . . and pulled. Ector moved forward to help him. Even with their combined strength the sword would not budge - even by an inch. 'Put your back into it,' said Ector angrily, but their efforts were useless.

'Let me at it,' said one of the knights, moving forward.

'Let's all have a turn,' murmured another.

'Here now, it's my turn,' said a third voice.

'Here . . . here . . . here. Stop pushing, all of you,' cried yet another.

The knights clustered eagerly round the sword in the stone, all trying in turn, none of them meeting with success. The black baron pushed his way through the crowd. 'Hold on, all of you. This isn't fair.'

'No, it isn't,' agreed Pelinore. 'I say let the boy try it.'

'Hear, hear. That's what I say. Give the lad a chance.' The black knight thrust Wart into the foreground.

'Go ahead, son,' urged Pelinore with a kindly smile. 'Try again.'

Wart's knees were trembling. Every eye was on him as he seized the hilt. The brilliant lights flashed as they had before and the air was a cadence of beautiful music. Once again the sword came away so easily that he fell backwards, still holding it. The crowds gasped their astonishment. It was incredible . . . a miracle. This slender slip of a boy had succeeded where the strongest in the land had failed.

A voice cried, *'It's a miracle ordained by heaven. This boy is our king.'*

Sir Ector and Kay looked more dumbfounded than anyone else. 'Well, by jove,' blustered Ector, remembering the long weary hours he had forced Wart to spend in the dank, underground kitchens, the hundreds of unjust demerits he had placed on the boy's head.

'What's the lad's name?' enquired the black baron, pleased by the turn of events.

'Wart! Oh . . . I mean Arthur,' blurted Ector, in some confusion.

The black baron held the boy's arm aloft, still bearing the famous sword. 'Hail . . . hail King Arthur!' he cried.

All the knights raised their swords in swift acknowledgement. 'Hail King Arthur!' The cry was taken up with enthusiasm all over the churchyard, and out into the crowded streets until the air all over London rang with the news. It spread like wildfire.

'Long live the King,' chanted the excited crowds. 'Long live the King!'

Archimedes flew into a nearby tree, shaking with mirth. 'Ho, ho, ho, ho . . . I can't believe it,' he chortled. But whether he could believe it or not, he was truly happy for his little charge and friend.

Sir Ector dropped to one knee to show his allegiance to the boy would soon be crowned king. 'Oh, forgive me, son . . . forgive me,' he pleaded.

'Oh, please don't, sir,' whispered Wart, in some embarrassment.

'Kay,' Ector ordered his rebellious sulky son. 'Bow down to your king!'

Reluctantly, Kay bent his knee.

CHAPTER ELEVEN

So at last the miracle had come to pass in that far off time upon New Year's Day, and the glorious reign of King Arthur was begun.

The long cold months of winter had fled and spring held the countryside cupped in gentle hands. The sun shone, the fields were green with fresh growth and the woods a patchwork of silver, lime and emerald with new quivering leaves. Warm-throated birds sang their songs of praise and the meadows showed promise of golden crops to come. Amidst the glory of the season, Wart too, was starting his new life. He was the king!

It was a strange role for the young lad and as he sat on the throne he looked round the great magnificent room with a sigh. His crown was a little large . . . he would have to grow. Pushing it back as it had fallen over his eyes, he turned to Archimedes who was never far away. 'I can't be king, Archimedes. I don't know anything about ruling a country.'

From his perch above the throne the owl looked down on his friend. 'I told you to leave the thing in the stone, boy.'

'I'll . . . I'll run away. That's what I'll do,' blurted out Wart, jumping down from the throne and removing his crown. 'They'll just have to get somebody else.'

The owl shrugged. He knew escape was impossible. The people loved the boy and were only too willing to show their trust and co-operation. 'Better take the side door, Wart,' advised the owl.

Dashing to the side door, Wart pulled it open. His face fell when he spied the waiting crowds. Raising a mighty cheer they called in unison, 'Hail King Arthur!'

Archimedes was going to fly out but the crowds were so thick that he turned back, cries of 'Long live the King', ringing in his sensitive ears. Wart slammed the door heavily and leaned against it.

'There's another door over there,' suggested Archimedes. 'Come on, try it!'

'Long live King Arthur,' greeted the boy and the bird when they peered out from the alternative exit. Archimedes shook his feathery head. 'Looks like we're surrounded, boy.'

Wart nodded miserable agreement. He felt trapped. It was a feeling he had known in the past in his lessons with the magician. 'Oh, Archimedes, I wish Merlin was here.' His voice was tinged with longing.

No sooner had he spoken than Merlin himself rocketed in through a slitted window, flew round the pillars, landed and skidded to a halt. Wart's eyes widened in wonder and happiness. 'Oh, Merlin . . . Merlin . . . you're back from Ber . . . Ber . . . ?'

'Bermuda,' prompted Merlin helpfully. 'Yes, I'm back from Bermuda and the twentieth century. Heh, heh! Believe me . . . you can have it.' Using his cane he changed his odd-looking garments from another era back to his usual purple robe and tall wizard's hat. 'That's better,' he said. 'The twentieth century is just one big modern mess. Ugh!'

'I'm in an awful pickle,' confessed Wart. 'I'm king!'

'Yes, he's king,' cut in Archimedes. 'He pulled the sword from the stone.'

Merlin laughed heartily and placed his arm about the boy's slim shoulders. 'Of course . . . *of course* he's king.' He led the boy back up the steps to the

throne. 'King Arthur and his Knights of the Round Table!' Merlin smiled then asked, 'Or would you rather have a square one?'

Wart laughed too, so great was his relief to have his dear friend and adviser once again at his side. He thought he had lost him for ever. 'Oh, no. A round one will be fine,' he answered.

Merlin picked up the gold crown set with fine jewels, placing it back on Wart's head. 'You'll become a great legend,' he promised. 'They'll be writing books about you for centuries to come.' The crown slipped forward but Merlin gently readjusted it. 'Why . . . they might even make a motion picture about you.'

'Motion picture?' queried Wart, not understanding the strange words.

Merlin smiled as Archimedes perched on the throne close to Wart. 'Well,' explained the magician, ' . . . that's something like television without commercials.'

Wart and the owl looked at each other and shrugged. 'Well, it doesn't matter now,' said Merlin. 'I can explain later!'

A beautifully illustrated,
intelligent appreciation of the
most popular artist of the age

THE ART OF
WALT DISNEY

FROM MICKEY MOUSE TO
THE MAGIC KINGDOMS

By Christopher Finch

Detailed biographical information on Disney, plus a thorough study of the history and techniques of animation, prepare the reader for a magical journey through the wonderful world of Disney.

Each well-known character is illustrated, there are stunningly-beautiful double-page spreads and pull-outs featuring stills from Disney films, and a comprehensive section on the Disney television specials and recreation parks.

With its pages of lavish illustrations, this highly-acclaimed hardcover book is the most complete visual and critical exploration of the world of Walt Disney ever published.

448 pages

© WALT DISNEY PRODUCTIONS

Available now at good booksellers everywhere, price £15.00

Should you have any difficulty in obtaining this book, please do not hesitate to write to the publishers, New English Library, at Barnard's Inn, Holborn, London EC1N 2JR

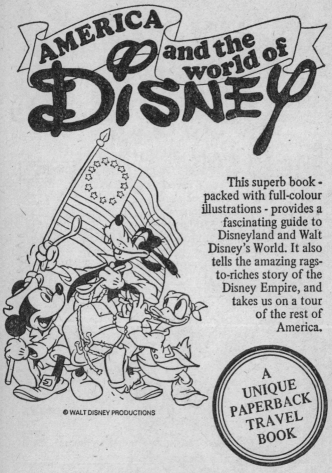

DONALD DUCK

the great Walt Disney weekly · 10p

You'll love this exciting
colour weekly with its
uproarious antics of Donald
and many of your
favourite Disney stars!
Be sure to get this feast of fun
every Thursday.